Pages from the Diary of A Geologist

Pages from the Diary of A Geologist

DR. G. S. SRIVASTAVA
**(Former Deputy Director General,
Geological Survey of India)**

PRABHAT
PRAKASHAN

Published by

PRABHAT PRAKASHAN PVT. LTD.

4/19 Asaf Ali Road,
New Delhi-110002 (INDIA)
e-mail: prabhatbooks@gmail.com

ISBN 978-93-5562-294-5

PAGES FROM THE DIARY OF A GEOLOGIST

by Dr. G. S. Srivastava (Former Deputy Director General, Geological Survey of India)

Edition
First, 2024

Price
₹ 400 (Rupees Four Hundred Only)

Printed at
SS Japan Art, Delhi

Dedicated to my team members and personal staff, Gurang Bahadur, Gulam Ahmad Bhat, Ram Kishan, Maya Ram, Khushal Singh and the mule walah Aziz Raina for their dedicated service rendered during different expeditions.

Author's Note

Perhaps I was born adventurous or the circumstances of my native village, Mau, a remote area in Rae Bareli district of Uttar Pradesh, where I was born, that made me adventurous. Since the age of 4 years we, a group of boys of a big joint family, used to go to our mango orchards at dawn to pick ripe mangos. Our village had only one Lower Primary School, which was run in the courtyard of our ancestral temple. After passing out of my second grade, I was forced to go to Upper Primary School at Rokha, located some three kilometres away from my village, on foot, in company of older boys of my village, indulging in all sorts of adventures and mischief. Once I was bitten by a scorpio and on another occasion, I slipped into a pond and nearly drowned.

For further schooling, I went to a Junior High School at Tekari, situated about seven kilometres away. This to and fro journey was also to be managed on foot, every day. I was accompanied by a few boys from my village. In course of time, I developed a liking for walking and trekking over long distances. Staying in a large house of my distant relative, all alone, self-cooking and attending a night school organised in a court of the princely state of Tekari, was a nightmarish experience.

Further higher secondary education was achieved at the Government Intermediate College, Rae Bareli, where I stayed with my maternal uncle. I was good at studies and was a pet of my mathematics and chemistry teachers. I scored fifty out of fifty in Chemistry in the half yearly examination of the college and my answer book was circulated among the Intermediate final aspirants of all the local colleges. However, I could not secure distinction (75%and above) in Chemistry in the final examination as I did in both Mathematics and Physics. I also secured the highest aggregate marks in the District.

Seeking admission in the University of Lucknow was an easy affair. However, I was averse to pursuing further studies in Chemistry and hence only two other combinations were available with Physics and Mathematics, namely Statistics or Geology. I had no idea of either of the subjects. Knowing that Statistics is like Mathematics, I filled up my admission form accordingly and stood in the queue at the cashier's office to deposit my fees. As providence had it, the boy just behind me looked at my form and suggested that Geology is a better option where you could go on tours to mountains of different regions of India during the course. I liked the idea instantaneously, wrote Geology in place of Statistics and deposited my fees. That is how, I became a graduate and postgraduate in Geology and eventually served the Geological Survey of India (GSI) later.

In my long years of service in GSI and other organisations, many adventurous incidents took place, especially during my field work in the Himalayas. Many were interesting and some were inspiring to the younger generation of geologists. My daughters were goading me to write about these, since they had heard the tales from me, every time I had returned back from my field work. I got the opportunity to do so at the tranquil and spacious house of my son at Southlake in Texas, USA. At that time, my granddaughter was introduced to English Writing through school and hence 'instructed' me on how to write 'Realistic Fiction'. I followed the pattern in some episodes, but narrated in my own way in others.

I hope the account of episodes will interest many readers, in general and the budding geologists in particular.

❑

Acknowledgments

I am grateful to my wife, Usha, for supporting me in this endeavour. Her undaunted spirit for caring the family, all alone during my long absence for field work in GSI, was a source of inspiration and kept me free from family worries for carrying out my researches. My elder daughter, Nidhi Khare, IAS, had gone through the manuscript and offered valuable comments and suggestions, despite her busy schedule. My son Ashish Shanker and daughter-in-law Dr. Shweta was a perfect host at their house in Southlake, Texas, where I had written a large part of the book. The concluding episodes were written at Nanded, Maharashtra, where my younger daughter Neeti Sarkar was posted as Divisional Railway Manager. Her suggestions were also incorporated to improve the manuscript of the book. Some of the initial sketches for the book were drawn by my granddaughter Samriddhi.

Contents

Author's Note 7

Acknowledgments 11

1 An Excursion in the Himalayas 17

2 Dhuandhar Waterfall at Bhera Ghat 21

3 Fire in an Oil Well at Rander 26

4 Ascent to a Hilltop 29

5 Visit to the Amarnath Cave 32

6 Camping in a Graveyard 34

7 Crossing of the Sind River 38

8 Winter in Srinagar 41

9 Pilgrimage to Vaishno Devi 47

10 Crossing of Chenab River for Lead Mines at Chichhe 52

11 Encounter with a King Cobra 56

12	On the Trail of a Bear	58
13	A Pair of Bears with a Cub	60
14	Serious Injury	62
15	Hill Diarrhoea	65
16	The Thrill of First Flight	69
17	First Paper Presentation in a Seminar	73
18	Visit of the Minister to Srinagar Office	77
19	Night with a Bakarwal Family	79
20	Travails of Ram Kishan	83
21	Bullfight on a Precipice	87
22	Selfless Service of Maya Ram	90
23	Reviving a Water Spring	92
24	Eye Drops	95
25	At the Base of Piparan Peak	97
26	Camp Shift to Singpur Gali	100
27	Maya Ram's Journey to Pathankot to See a Train	103
28	Leap of a Tiger	106
29	Traversing through a Synclinal Closure off Rathwadhab	110
30	Field Work in the Teruel Province of Spain	113
31	Professor's Visit	118

32 An Episode in Rome 121

33 Cat in a Paris Hotel 124

34 Menace of Honey Bees 127

35 Caught up in a Storm 130

36 Field Check in Sahibi Basin of Haryana 133

37 Snowfall at Manali 137

38 Jeep Accident 141

39 Ceremonial Parade at Srinagar 144

40 Snakebite in Nagarjuna Sagar Area 147

41 Crossing of an Icefan Near Chandanwari 149

42 Aerial Photography of Gola Catchment Area 152

43 Enquiry in a Geophysical Work Contract 155

44 Altercation between Two Scientists 158

45 Dadua Gang Episode 161

46 Night Halt in a Village House 164

47 Meeting an Old Classmate at Madawara 168

48 Negotiating a Damaged Road Near Bijawar 171

49 An Incident with Mr Jero at Pushkar 174

50 New Map Policy 177

51 Convincing the Honourable Minister 180

52 Visiting Professorship in Bundelkhand University 185
53 Digitization of Data in an Irrigation Department 188
54 Anomalous Water Divide of Bata and Markanda Rivers 191
55 The Enigma of Lost Saraswati River at Prayag Raj 196
56 Nepal Earthquake of April 2015 200
57 Changes in Survey Techniques 204

❑

1

An Excursion in the Himalayas

An excursion was planned in the Ranikhet-Almora-NainiTal area in the Lesser Himalayas by the Geology Department of University of Lucknow in May-June, 1960 after our examinations of B. Sc. (previous) that year. NainiTal was connected to Lucknow by a metre gauge railway up to Kath Godam. Beyond the rail head, one has to travel by road to reach aforementioned places in the Himalaya. We, the students of Geology, boarded the NainiTal Express in the evening of the appointed date, carrying our holdalls. There were no sleeper class bogies on the train at that time. It had first, second and third classes. Our teachers, Mr Girjesh Chandra and Mr S. K. Singh, were travelling in first class, while a few girl students with their guardians were travelling in second class and the rest of us were travelling in third class. As students we were entitled for half fare and being members of a party, a bogey was allotted to us, where generally no other passengers were allowed to board. So we spread our holdalls on the seats of our bogey and made ourselves comfortable. As it was hot in Lucknow, we used our *razais* (cotton quilt), which we were carrying with us to obviate the cold climate of the hills, as a cushion.

We slept rather late in the evening, but slept well, after having frivolous discussions, joking, laughing and exchanging pleasant experiences acquired during our short summer vacation at our homes. When we got up in the morning, it was Lal Kuan railway station. We saw a faint skyline of a mountain range, though still far away. It was thrilling to most of us coming from the vast Ganga plain. I had not seen a mountain till then. By the time we reached Haldwani, the forest-clad Himalayan foothills with snowy peaks in the background, became clearly visible. We reached the last railway station Kath Godam by about 10 AM. It was cold there and therefore, most of us took out our half sweaters. After having breakfast, we boarded our bus for the onward journey to Ranikhet. As soon as the bus entered the hill section, the road started winding and appeared very narrow. As we ascended, we felt scared on every turn of the road, apprehensive that we were likely to fall into the deep ravine. Many of us felt giddy and started vomiting. I also vomited. Our classmates, Harish Chandra Pant and Gajendra Singh

Pundeer, who were from Kumaon and Garhwal regions of the Himalayan hills of Uttar Pradesh, respectively, advised us that we should keep looking outside the windows, while the bus is moving on the winding road, so that the coordination with the hills would be maintained. This practice helped us a lot and I followed it thoughout the fieldwork in mountains during the years ahead in the Geological Survey. We reached Garam Pani in the afternoon, where we had lunch and a good break from the bus journey.

We reached Ranikhet in the evening and settled in the hall of the hotel booked for us. It was quite cold and we were tired. So we had early dinner to go to the cosy *razai* for a sound sleep. When we woke up the next morning, it was already daybreak. Two or three of my friends hurriedly went out with our mug and water bottles for the morning call. I moved along the slope for some distance, when I suddenly slipped on pine leaves and fell in a ditch about fifteen feet below. Luckily the ditch was filled with pine leaves and so I escaped without sustaining any major injury. My friends helped me to come out of the ditch to a plain area and tried to restore my confidence. We learnt the second lesson, again from my friends from the hills, that we should negotiate a hill slope in a zig-zag manner and not move directly along the slope line. After breakfast, we all took our geological traverse toward Mukteshwar, now moving in a zig-zag manner and with much confidence. This lesson also kept me in good stead while working in the challenging mountainous terrains in future.

The initial traverse was very tiring, though the next three four days of work made us strong enough to move on the hill slopes with ease, while observing different rocks and minerals occurring in the area. We moved on to Ram Garh, Almora and NainiTal subsequently, to complete our excursion. We collected many samples of rocks and minerals and also collected some good looking rounded pebbles from the very clear water stream beds as a souvenir.

❑

2

Dhuandhar Waterfall at Bhera Ghat

As part of the curriculum for B. Sc. (Final) students, the Geology Department of Lucknow University organised an excursion in Jabalpur Area for us during Dussehra - Deewali holidays of 1960, to familiarise with the sedimentary rocks of Vindhyan and Gondwana super groups and volcanic rocks of Deccan Traps. We in a batch of some thirty students left Lucknow by train in the evening and reached Maihar in the early hours of the next day. We settled down in a Dharmashala. Our staff became active and no sooner we performed our morning chorus, we got our morning tea. Soon we got ready for field work and had our breakfast of *poori bhaji.* We trecked along a nala section and examined the rocks of Vindhyan Supergroup, which comprised sandstone, shale and limestone. Our teachers showed us many features of geological interest. A headcount was made at the end of our traverse when we reached on the road and reached our camp (Dharmashala) by late afternoon to enjoy *Tahri* prepared by our staff.

After resting for a while, we went for a darshan of Maihar Devi temple, situated at the top of a hill about a thousand feet above the ground. Though there were steps for going to the temple, most of us preferred climbing along the foot track in our enthusiasm and skill acquired during the day while taking a geological traverse. The temple has the main deity of Bundela heroes Alha- Udal, whose exploits of bravery are sung in Bundelkhand and Awadh regions of Uttar Pradesh and Madhya Pradesh. The famous musician Ustad Allauddin Khan used to practiced and perform *Sitar Vadan* at the temple.

Next day, we went to Katni, a town known for coal mining activity. We visited Chirmiri coal mine nearby. The coal is occurring in Gondwana rocks having a sequence of sandstone, shale and coal but no limestone as these rock are laid in fresh waters. We did not go inside the coal mine, however, our teachers explained different stages of formation of coal from vegetative matter to peat then to lignite. Further confinement under pressure for prolonged period leads to formation of bituminous coal, which is mostly used as fuel in homes and industry including railways. More intense pressure may leads to formation of Anthracite, a kind of coal used in steel industry. The bituminous coal taken out from the mines are stacked in the vast railway yard for taking it to different places. The notable thing after Katni trip was that our clothes and shoes were soiled black.

The next day we travelled to Jabalpur by bus and reached there in the afternoon. We made ourselves comfortable in the hall of a hotel, located on the outskirts of the city, not far from Chhui Hill, where we went the next day. Chhui Hill is made up of limestone which got thermally metamorohosed into chalk, locally called chhuhi, which is used for writing on a blackboard in a classroom. The chalk limestone is being mined for that purpose. There was a classic gravity fault exposed in the face of the mine clearly showing the displacement of rocks on either side of the fault line. We observed other geological features in the locality. In the afternoon, we went to see Madan Mahal, a ruined abode of Rani Durgavati, who valiantly fought and repulsed the Moghul Army a couple of times till Emperor Akbar himself led the battle front. She fought fiercely and sacrificed her life in the battle. There is also the famous balancing rock present in the area. It is a huge granite boulder resting on a granite block. The boulder had remained stationary for thousands of years despite many storms and earthquakes occurring in the area.

We went to Chhota Nagpur Hill the next day. The hill comprised volcanic rocks of Deccan Trap. It is full of volcanic features showing gas cavities, which later filled with mineralizing solutions to develop different varieties of quartz crystals, prominent among these are amethyst and agate. We were thrilled to collect such beautiful samples. Subsequently, we went to Dhuandhar Water Fall located in Bhera Ghat area. It is in the marble rocks exposed across Narmada River. The huge water mass of the river falls in a shear drop of about 100 feet, creating mist and the roaring sound, which is heard from a good distance all around. The river being perennial in nature, the waterfall runs throughout the year. Some people enjoyed boating trips down the stream. The marble rocks are soft due to magnesium content, hence are extensively used for carving of various figures popular among the tourists coming from all over India. The soap stone available in this locality is also used for carving. We enjoyed the site for nearly the whole afternoon, though constantly forbidden by our teachers not to venture in the river for causing any mishap. We had our headcounts again at the end of the trip before returning to our camp.

We went to Balaghat Manganese Mines on the last day our excursion. It was an open cast mine in metamorphic rocks of Archaean age. The mineral occurs in oxide, carbonate and sulphate forms. The crystals were back and generally soiled our hands. We collected some samples of the ore as well as the host rock. We were back to Jabalpur in the evening to catch our train in the night. The load of the rock samples was gradually reduced as more and more samples were collected in each subsequent camp. Finally, on reaching Lucknow, we kept the samples in our laboratory, for selection of the better ones to be displayed in our Museum. I carried the quartz and agate samples to show these to our cousins at Rae Bareli, who were equally thrilled. My maternal grandmother was so happy to see these beautiful crystals that she remarked that I should better make a necklace pendant with the quartz and amethyst crystals for my wife in future.

❑

3

Fire in an Oil Well at Rander

After completing my Master's Degree in Geology, I was selected as Senior Technical Assistant in the Oil Natural Gas Commission (ONGC) and was posted at Bharuch in Gujarat, in March 1964. My job was to examine rockchips coming out of the oil wells and attend to the wildcat drilling going on in the Ankaleshwar oilfield, located between the Narmada and Tapti rivers. After about a year, I was transferred to Rander, close to Surat, across the Tapti River. Here, I was assigned to a deep exploration drilling being carried out with a Romanian rig. The well was targeted to drill down to a depth of more than 4000 metres. When I joined the team in June '65, the drilling of the well went smoothly till the cementation of the first casing, but after that there were shutdowns due to some problem or the other..

The drilling resumed and reached down to a depth of 1300 metres. Suddenly, one day there was a gas blowout. The pipes of drilling string were thrown out and there were intermittent explosions of mud and gas. The days were hot and the well caught fire, perhaps due to collision of drilling pipes in one of the explosions. The oil well became a big pit with a burning flame. It was impossible to go near the well and attempt capping of the well. The matter turned very serious and it was immediately reported to the regional headquarters at Baroda, who in turn informed the Central Headquarters at Dehra Dun. Soon we had a meeting with the Resident Geologist from Bharuch, who had rushed to Rander in the meanwhile. It was decided that we carry out detailed mapping surrounding the wellsite and suggest a location far away from the drill site, for making an inclined drill hole to connect the oil well at a reasonably deeper level. This had to be very precise work.

The next day we started plane table surveying starting from a point as close to the well as possible, up to about 500 metres away on the periphery. We completed this task in a couple of days, working in two shifts from sunrise to sunset, thanks to the longer days. We plotted the map during the night. The spot for the inclined hole and its angle, etcetera were decided in the meeting of experts, on the subsequent day and the shallow drilling machine also arrived the next day. The drilling for an inclined hole began soon and in three four days, we intersected the oil well. We were jubilant over this success and appreciated the expertise of the drilling team as well. This hole was capped so that flow of gas and mud could be regulated.

A fire fighting team was called in. It was coordinated with the cementing unit based at Ankleshwar. The next day about eight tankers with water and fire extinguishing fluid arrived at the well site. The plan was that the cap of the inclined hole would be opened in between two successive explosions to reduce the gas pressure of the burning oil well. Simultaneously, the water and fire extinguishing fluid was to be directed at the burning oil well. The action started by 4 PM, when day temperature declined and the atmosphere became more humid with wind blowing in from the sea. The flame went out in the middle of the operation. We waited in grim silence for the next explosion, which occurred in about 30 seconds. But this time there was no flame and only gas charged mud came out with low intensity. All of us present at the well site started shouting with joy and hugging each other in frenzy for achieving the success.

The arrangements were made to cap the main oil well. The inclined hole was also shut down and a paid holiday was declared the next day, much to the relief of everybody.

❑

4

Ascent to a Hilltop

I joined the Jammu and Kashmir Circle of Geological Survey of India (GSI) as Assistant Geologist in June, 1966 at Srinagar. After completing initial formalities and preparations, I was dispatched to join the Sind[1] Valley Expedition led by Mr S. P. Rastogi, who was senior to me in the University of Lucknow as well as in the GSI. We started our first camp in Sonamarg, situated at a height of about 7000 feet above mean sea level. I started learning the basics of geological mapping. It also involved learning of

---

1 Although pronounced as 'Sindh', this river is different than Indus River. Sind River is a smaller river flowing through Baltal, Sonamarg, Kangan and Gandarbal, contributing to Jhelum River Basin.

the fundamentals of mountaineering in high altitude areas, which are as follows:

1. Acclimatise for a couple days, taking reconnaissance traverses.
2. Go slow while climbing up or climbing down.
3. Keep pace and do not take frequent rests.
4. While resting, do not take off the jacket, only zip off or zip up as the need be.
5. Fluid intake should be at a higher level.

We started practising these rules and carried out mapping on the southern face of Sind Valley around Sonamarg. After about 8 days we shifted our camp to the next valley to continue mapping further. One day we decided to climb a hill top in search of Jurassic rocks likely to be there. The day was clear and sunny. The hilltop looked so close that we thought that we could climb up and return back by the afternoon. So we started climbing.

It took almost three hours to reach the base of the summit. The summit was not as near as it looked. The slope was steeper. Our guide coolies advised us not to venture further as it was past noon. However, Mr Rastogi was adamant to proceed further. I simply followed him. The coolies sat at the base and refused to accompany us. We started climbing up the slope carefully and slowly. It took almost two hours of rigorous effort to make it to the summit. To our dismay, we did not get any Jurassic rocks. The Triassic Limestone continued right up to the summit. Suddenly, clouds appeared on the horizon. The clouds covered the summit sooner than we thought. We started climbing down. It was not easy to move down the steep slope. It started snowing and the slope became slippery and thus all the more difficult to move down. We slipped here and there but clinged to the rock joints and juniper bushes to save our lives. Moving further was possible only on all fours. Luckily, the snow stopped after half an hour. We continued moving downwards laboriously. At long last, we reached the base of the summit in another two hours, completely battered. The guide coolies were nowhere around. They had run away to safety in view of the impending hailstorm. The dusk was approaching and we were too hungry. So we opened our lunch boxes and ate. In the meanwhile, the guide coolies located us and came to our rescue. We reached our camp somehow, taking their support for the remaining distance.

The lessons learnt from this episode are:

1. Do not underestimate the hill tops. They appear to be at a shorter distance and at a lower height than they actually are.
2. Start early for climbing to the summit. The afternoons are generally cloudy and it may rain or snow.
3. Examine the 'float' (apron rocks) carefully to ascertain the rocks occurring at the top.

❑

5

Visit to the Amarnath Cave

After some time, we shifted our camp to Baltal, a place located on the right bank of Sind River. The area to be mapped was on the left bank. There was a snow bridge available upstream and therefore, we mapped the lower reaches of the left face of Sind River passing over the bridge every time. Amarnath Cave, located at about 14000 feet above mean sea level, was not very popular as a major pilgrimage centre in those days. Hindu pilgrims in groups visited the holy cave for a few days around Shravan Purnima in the month of August, through the Pahalgam-Panjtarni route. Our guide coolies told us that a footpath leads to the holy cave from Baltal, though the climb is steep in the first half of the journey. So we decided to visit the holy cave on the auspicious day of Shravan Purnima, a couple of days later.

On the appointed day, we left our camp early in the morning. We negotiated a steep slope by moving slowly and steadily through the zigzag foot path. Occasionally, we had to negotiate narrow stretches. However, we finished the steeper part of the journey by 11: 00 am. The remaining part of the journey was along a gentler path extending for a distance of about four kilometres. We reached the holy cave at about 2:00 pm, walking over several snow beds across the streams en route. It was quite cold inside the cave and sitting there barefoot for puja was an ordeal. However, we had darshan of the Ice Lingam of Lord Shiva and performed Puja. We were exalted.

After the Darshan, we sat on a rock outcrop in the sun and ate our packed lunch. We left the cave area around 3:00 pm. The return journey was at a faster pace, as climbing down was much easier. We reached our camp by 7:30 pm before it was too dark, very tired though highly satisfied. For me, it was all the more satisfying as this was my first Field-Season's work in GSI and I had the Darshan of the holy cave of Amarnath.

❑

6

Camping in a Graveyard

After about a week, we again shifted our camp deep in the valley of the stream joining Sind River on the left bank, opposite Baltal. We used the snow bridge for crossing the Sind River, taking all the bags and baggage on the mules to the left bank and then to the new camping site up the stream. We had planned to map the whole face up to the ridge and then to cross over through the Kolahoi pass located at the head of the stream to Pahalgam side. Our camp was situated at about 11000 feet above mean sea level. It was middle of September and we could safely carry out mapping work till the end of September before it snows. So we started our geological traverses regularly.

On 22nd September '66, we took a traverse upstream almost up to the Kolahoi ridge. We located a beautiful lake at the base of Kolahoi Mountain. It was a fascinating site having deep blue waters surrounded by snowy mountains on three sides. We stayed at the shore of the lake for a while and had our lunch. We returned back to our camp late in the afternoon. The sky was still clear and sunny. Suddenly our labourer mate came to us, informing us that we must shift our camp tomorrow downstream as it is likely to snow here. We were surprised at his prediction and brushed aside his advice, as it had been a sunny day all through. He persistently told us that the mules were sniffing the moisture in the atmosphere. We told the mule wallahs that only one day's work is left and the day after we may cross the Kolahoi ridge to a safer place on the other side.

After an early dinner, we zipped ourselves in the sleeping bags in the tent and slept. Very early in the next morning, I felt that our tent was sagged and was very close to my chest. When I lifted it with the help of my ice axe, I heard the thud of falling snow mass accumulated on the flaps of our tent. I awakened Mr Rastogi. We crawled out of the tent to see the snow all around us. It was very bright and not so cold out there. We called our cook Gurang Bahadur to get some hot tea and asked the peon to clear the snow near the portals of all tents. When we came out of our tent, we noticed that all the mules had run away in the night for a safe place downstream.

The labour mate, Aziz Raina, was an experienced old person. He asked four or five mule wallahs to go downstream in search of the mules. With the help of the remaining two guys, he started clearing the path which was covered by the recent snowfall. This operation virtually lasted for the whole day and to our good luck the weather remained clear. In the evening the mule wallas reported that they could locate their mules herded below a tree. After taking their meals early, they took one tent and went to camp near the mules. It was decided that we would shift our camp to some suitable place downstream, the next day. We prayed that it would not snow during the night and slept. Next day was cloudy but it did not rain or snow. We had our breakfast and got our lunch packed. The tents and other equipment were packed. The mule wallas brought the mules with difficulty as the mules were reluctant to climb up. However, we could start shifting our camp only in the afternoon. The kitchen tent with Gurang Bahadur moved first with the instruction that he should find a flat ground for pitching our tents near a drinking water source. Gurang Bahadur reached Baz Khoran, a place close to the confluence of the stream with Sindh River and pitched his tent and started preparing food for dinner. After a while we also reached the site and asked the labourers to pitch our tents and another tent for the labourers. By the time they finished the job, it was dark. Bahadur served us a hot cup of tea, which was very welcome. Soon we laid our air mattresses over the boxes and spread the sleeping bags over it. The petromax kept inside the tent (a double fly shouldary) kept it warm. The dinner was served and we retired soon thereafter.

Next morning after drinking tea, I came out of the tent to see the area around. Bahadur suddenly came rushing to me to tell me that the ice bridge over Sindh River had broken during the recent rains. He also told me that he had spotted a lone sheep caught between the broken ice pieces. He wanted to kill the sheep to get meat for all of us. I told him to take Aziz Raina in confidence and do whatever he said.

Suddenly, I noticed that the ground where tents are pitched is uneven and had many low mounds all over. It had a typical weed grown over the mounds. I then realised that our tents are pitched in a graveyard. The mounds were the graves and the weed, a kind of white lily, grown over them further testified my surmise. Mr Rastogi also concurred with my views. Now, what is to be done? We discussed the alternatives. In view of the fact that we must shift our camp across the Sind River in a day or two, we decided to let the camp be there itself. After all, we had tea, dinner and slept last night peacefully, the fear of staying in a graveyard had vanished altogether.

❑

7

Crossing of the Sind River

I had a sumptuous lunch that day as Bahadur had prepared and served meat dishes. Mr Rastogi, being a vegetarian, was surprised at this. Bahadur narrated the whole story about finding the lone sheep and managing it with the help of Aziz Raina. He also said that part of the meat was stored in the snow bed for future consumption. The rest was given to the labourers and they had a heyday.

In the meanwhile, Aziz Raina surveyed the whole area and reported about his plans for crossing the Sind River. Since the snow bridge, through which we came, got shattered during the recent rains, a temporary foot-bridge was to be constructed over the river to ferry out men, mules and camp equipment. Raina had located two big boulders in the river bed. He went to the nearby forest and located two big fallen pine trees to be used as beams for the foot bridge. Cutting trees or using fallen logs was prohibited as it was a reserved forest. There was no way of communicating to the Forest Officer for securing his permission in this regard. Under the circumstances, it was decided that we request for a post facto permission to use the two pine trees to meet the emergency requirement, while performing government duty. We asked Raina and their labourer companions to bring the pine trees to the campsite along with their branches. They finished the job by the evening.

The operation 'Foot Bridge' started early next morning. The water flow in the river is somewhat reduced in the early hours of the morning due to freezing of water upstream. That is why Raina decided to finish the beam work in the morning hours. We went slightly upstream above the two boulders located earlier in the river bed. A nylon rope was tied to one end of the beam. Every one of us held the rope and the beam was allowed to flow in the river channel. It went like an arrow in the river water. We guided the beam in such a manner that it rested against boulders. Two labourers along with Raina and Bahadur went up to the first boulder and lifted the beam onto it. Using the boulder as fulcrum, they somehow put the other end of the beam on the next boulder. Now the question was who should move on the beam first to reach to the other boulder. It was a hazardous task and needed courage to do that. Finally Bahadur volunteered to do the job. Holding the ice axe horizontally by both hands and balancing his body on the beam, he cautiously moved on the beam and reached the other end successfully. We were watching this feat in stupefied silence on this side of the river. We sighed with relief to see Bahadur triumphantly standing on the other boulder. Repeating the same feat with the second beam was much simpler. In the afternoon session, the branches were cut into two foot logs. Each log was further cut longitudinally into two flat pieces. These pieces were tied to the two beams with grass rope like a close spaced ladder. And lo! The footbridge was ready.

First of all, the mules were taken to the other side of the river, one by one, guided by their respective mule wallah. The bridge was repaired here and there after this operation, to make it passable for the labourers with camp equipment. We two officers were last to leave to see that nothing was left behind. When we reached our new camp near Baltal, we wrote two letters; one to the Forest Officer for using two fallen pine trees and the other to the Superintending Geologist, J. & K. Circle, at Srinagar for permitting us to close our camp, as it was nearing the end of the Field-Season and no further work was possible.

❑

8

Winter in Srinagar

After closing our camp, we returned back to our headquarters at Srinagar, in the first week of October '66. Soon, other expedition parties arrived. My friend and room partner Mr Bir Singh had also returned back from Ladakh. The offices of Jammu and Kashmir Government are stationed at Jammu during the winter and at Srinagar during the summer months. The Government staff moved to Jammu in November and back to Srinagar in May. This movement was prevalent since the pre-independence days of Maharaja Hari Singh, and was popularly known as 'Darbar Movement'. The term is still being used for the periodic shifting of the Government Offices in J. & K.

State. There was a move to follow the same pattern for Central Government Offices as well. However, it did not materialise till then. Therefore, we were to stay in Srinagar during the winter.

We had moved to a new flat in Jawahar Nagar, as the rents became cheaper during the winter due to less occupancy. The families in the adjoining flats had gone to Jammu on Darbar Move in the first week of November. We requested our landlord to allow us to occupy the flat on the ground floor due to the impending winter. He readily agreed and we shifted to a ground floor apartment which was more comfortable. We settled in a single room, having a heating device called Bukhari, placed in the centre of the room and our cots beside it. We used to cook our breakfast and lunch in the adjoining kitchen and had packed lunch for the office, which was located in Rajbagh, not far off. The days were shorter; the sunrise was at 7:30 am while the sunset was at 5:00 pm, which further shifted to a 7:45 am to 4:30 pm span by the end of December.

There was no central heating system in the office. The rooms were kept warm by burning wood in bukhari's kept in each room. The work in the office was light. Besides the routine office work, we were engaged in consultation of geological literature in the library and writing reports for the work carried out in the previous Field-Season. On sunny days, during lunch break, we used to cross the Jhelum River by Shikara to visit Ahdoo's coffee shop, located on the bund on the opposite side. These short sessions were utilized in exchanging our experiences, good and bad, during our field trips. Occasionally, the discussions turned into intellectual exchanges, which were quite lively, especially when it was between Mr Wakhloo and Mr Rastogi.

By the end of November, the weather became inclement and the temperature started lowering day by day. The leaves of chinar, poplar and walnut trees started turning orange, red and brown. The whole valley looked very colourful and picturesque. After a while the trees started shedding their leaves, preparing for the severe winter ahead. Srinagar had its first snowfall of the season in the first week of December. It was pleasantly cold while it snowed, due to the emission of latent heat. Afterwards, it became quite cold. When Office was closed by 4:30 pm, it was already dark. After a brief stroll through Lal Chowk, we used to have our early dinner in a Jammu Dhaba (owned by a Sharma ji), located near Amira Kadal bridge. On our way back, we often collected groceries for the next day.

On one of these days, it started snowing in the evening. We stayed in the office for a while but the situation did not improve. Ultimately, we left the office with an overcoat and fur cap on, while it still was snowing. We reached our residence quickly and went inside the bed. After resting for a while we lit the bukhari and took some hot tea with some toasts and boiled eggs. It was still snowing and we decided not to venture out for dinner. We did not feel hungry at that moment and decided to sleep. After a couple of hours of sleep, suddenly, we felt very hungry and we were wide awake. As there was no bread left in the house, we took one packet of biscuits each and consumed it. We drank some warm water and slept again. Next day, we procured bread and eggs from a nearby bakery shop and found that there was about a foot of snow all around. Our water taps were frozen and there were rods of ice from the tap to the ground. We took these rods of ice and heated them in a vessel to get some water for our cooking. We had prepared lunch quickly and ate, while packing the egg and toast for the office. Fortunately, the snow had stopped by the time we left for our office.

It was nearing the end of December and we thought of organising a new year eve party. Mr Alam volunteered to have the party at his residence as his family had gone back to his native place, Jaunpur in Uttar Pradesh. He actually belonged to a Nawab family of Jaunpur and a touch of royalty reflected in his behaviour. An accomplished cook, Riaz was his personal domestic help. It was a contributory dinner while the drinks were offered by the host. A card game was also planned prior to the dinner. We, about six or seven friends, assembled at Mr Alam's place in Jawahar Nagar at about 7:00 PM. We were served with light snacks and hot tea. Soon we were engrossed in the card game with munchings in between. Mr Dhall and Mr Kapur were the usual winners on such occasions. However, this time it was the turn of Mr Mathur and Mr Bir Singh. We enjoyed the game thoroughly, while the transistor radio provided necessary background music and songs of contemporary films. The card game lasted till about midnight when we hailed the happy new year by toasting it and greeting each other. Soon the dinner was laid. Thc main dish was 'Ran Musallam' prepared by the accomplished chef Riaz, using a variety of spices. The dish was very delicious. It was prepared out of the whole rear leg of a goat, cooked on slow fire. We ate it to our heart's content with chapatis and pulao. Mr Alam was a voracious eater. He bade us goodbye, while still holding the femur bone by both the hands and a stack of chapati column measuring about four inches high, waiting to be devoured.

In the first week of January in 1967, the weather worsened with more snow . The minimum temperature of Srinagar dipped to about minus 8 degree celsius. We had not taken a bath for the last fifteen days or so. Mr Bir Singh located a 'Hammam' in Lal Chowk area. It provided hot water bath rooms at a cost of Rs. two per head per bath. One had to carry his towel and soap. So, on the next Sunday we went there and had a good shower. One had to wear warm clothes like jacket, muffler, gloves, fur cap and overcoat etc., before coming out of the bathroom to get protection from the chill outside.

At the office, our reports were nearing completion, except the part related to petrological studies of rock samples collected during the fieldwork. The facilities for such studies were available only in our Petrological Laboratory at Jammu office. Hence, we requested our Superintending Geologist to permit us to proceed to Jammu for carrying out the laboratory studies. We were provided with a jeep to carry our rock samples. I was permitted to stay in the office premises, provided that I would not claim any allowances for my stay at Jammu. We readily agreed to this condition, in order to get rid of the severe winter of Srinagar.

Mr Bir Singh and I packed our baggage early in the morning and loaded it in the jeep trailer, where rock samples were already kept the previous evening. We left Srinagar around 8:30 AM. The snow had accumulated all along the road. There was up to five feet of snow on either side of the road near Qazigund. As soon as we came out of the Jawahar tunnel on the Banihal side, the temperature difference was like ten degrees. It was so pleasant near Banihal village, although the temperature there was like three degrees Celsius. We reached Jammu in the evening, where it looked like a warm evening, whereas the locals felt it was quite cold.

❑

9

Pilgrimage to Vaishno Devi

I was married in February 1967 and my wife, Usha, came with me to Jammu soon after. The Holi festival was in the third week of March, but that year, it rained for three days continuously. There was no playing of colours associated with the Holi festival and we remained confined to our house. When it cleared up, we saw the Trikuta hills covered with snow. These hills are visible from Jammu and Vaishno Devi Temple is located just below these hills. The shrine was popular among the devotees from Punjab and Delhi. It was not a popular destination for the people from other parts of India. In those days, the railway line was only up to Pathankot in Punjab. The onward journey to any place in the state of Jammu and Kashmir had to be performed by road. Sealdah-Pathankot Express was the main train connecting West Bengal, Bihar, Uttar Pradesh and Punjab to the J. & K. State.

The weather improved gradually, after the Holi holiday. It became sunny and pleasant. Being a newlywed couple, my landlady implored us to go for a Darshan of Mata Vaishno Devi during Navratri (a fortnight after Holi). So, we decided to make the trip to Vaishno Devi Temple during the second Saturday and Sunday of April. We left Jammu by bus on Friday afternoon, reaching Katra by 4:00 PM, a distance of about 50 km. The bus stopped at Nandini tunnel, en route, for tea break. The cheese pakoras of Nandini were quite famous in those days and we enjoyed the delicacy over a cup of tea. At Katra, which is located at the base of Trikuta hills, we procured mountaineering shoes and sticks on rent, for climbing the hill. We left Katra by about 4:30 PM and started climbing the stairs. Soon we realised that it is easier to move along the zigzag path, although it was longer in distance. After climbing for about two hours, sometimes by stairs and mostly along the footpath, we reached Ardhkuwari. It was getting dark and we decided to stay there for the night. Many people did that. Blankets were available for a nominal rent. We secured a place for ourselves in the Dormitory Hall built by the Shrine Board and slept there after having a light dinner.

There is a holy cave at Ardhkuwari having a narrow portal, such that only one person can descend at a time. We visited this cave the next morning. Once we passed through the portal, descending down, we reached a spacious hall, where idols of Mata ji are kept for Darshan. The portal again narrows while coming out of the cave. The shrine board regulates the entry of pilgrims, allowing only a group of six persons at a time, in order to avoid suffocation inside the cave. After Darshan of Ardhkuwari cave, we had our breakfast and started climbing further up. It was a clear sunny morning and we could see the meandering Chenab River at a far distance. The downhill precipices had scanty trees and looked fearsome. Usha was quite scared to look at those slopes. She preferred the forest laden gentler slopes on the other side. The climb of Hathi Mattha was tough. As noon was approaching, the last leg of climb to Bhairon Ghati was equally tough. We did not go to Bhairon Temple, as it is customary to have Darshan here after performing puja at Vaishno Devi Temple. We took the side path, which was even and after moving for a short distance, we started seeing the valley of Peyi Khad, the stream coming out of Vaishno Devi Caves. We rested for a while and then started moving gently downwards to reach the shrine. We took a room at the inn, kept our belongings there and left to have a bath in the stream water coming from the cave. The water was very cold initially but enjoyable afterwards.

The portal of the holy cave was nearby. It was bigger than the portal at Ardhkuwari but not big enough to walk in. One had to enter the cave by crawling. It was dark and cool inside and one had to wade through knee deep water. We were scared to enter and were chanting Jai Mata di involuntarily. After the portal, it became roomy enough to stand in the water and move further. After about 100 metres, the lights of the cave temple were visible. The cave became more spacious. Three well decorated idols (pindis) were visible in the light of a constantly burning oil lamp. We bowed our heads in reverence and offered flowers and other materials before the idols. The priest bestowed us with prasad and khajana with blessings from Mata Ji. After Darshan, we returned back by the same route. Our eyes now were more accustomed to seeing in the dark. We started seeing the other idols en route, which were supposed to be of Pandavas. After our batch of pilgrims came out of the cave, the next batch was allowed to go inside.

Evening was approaching, so we had Puris for our lunch-cum-dinner, followed by a hot cup of tea and slept early wrapped under the cosy blankets. The bathing had reduced our fatigue and a good night's rest further reduced it. We got up fresh next morning and started our return journey after having our breakfast. The climb up to Bhairon Temple was somewhat tiring. After Darshan at this temple, we rested for a while and enjoyed the scenic beauty of the surrounding area, as this was the highest point of the journey. The rest of the journey was moving downhill, which we covered leisurely. We had our lunch at Ardhkuwari and rested there for a while. By the evening we had reached Katra, content but very tired. At the inn at Katra, I arranged for some hot water and salt. It was very soothing to keep our feet in the warm salt water.

That eased our walking to some extent, although we were still limping due to excessive fatigue.

We stayed at the inn for the night. We could walk with difficulty to a nearby Dhaba for our dinner and deposited back the mountaineering shoes and sticks, on our way back to the inn. After a good night's rest, we felt better and took a bus to Jammu. We finally reached our residence in Gandhinagar in the afternoon. It took a couple of days for both of us to recover from the fatigue of climbing the hill.

❑

10

Crossing of Chenab River for Lead Mines at Chichhe

As a young Geologist of Geological Survey of India in 1967, I was assigned to carry out geological mapping, around an old lead mine at Chichhe in Kishtwar area of Jammu and Kashmir, under the guidance of a senior colleague Mr B. K. Dhruva Rao. After spending some time in the initial survey work, we decided to cross the Chenab River, as the lead mines were located on the other side of the river at the head of a scarp, at an altitude of 11000 feet. The river was highly turbulent and ferocious. There were no bridges on the river except a trolley bridge, which too was in a dilapidated condition. We were scared to cross the roaring river but there was no alternative.

After some discussion as to who should go on the first trip, we finally decided that both of us, along with our cash bags, should move first to cross the river. We sat in the trolley with two labourers sitting in the front to hold the iron rope. The trolley moved on the two iron wires like a bogey of a train. The first half of the journey along the sagging curve of iron wire was fast. The trolly reached over the middle of the river, which was very turbulent and roaring. The two labourers, sitting in the front, grabbed the iron wire by hand and started pulling the trolley upwards. Initially, the trolley went up smoothly due to its momentum, but later on it required a lot of effort to pull it up. At long last, the trolley reached the other bank of the river. They held the rope tight and asked us to jump off the trolley one by one. We did it very carefully and thus we reached the other side of the Chenab River, jubilant and relieved.

The labourers went back and ferried the camp equipment and other men one by one, through several trips. At the end of the day, all tents, rations and other survey equipment were shifted to the right bank of Chenab River. In the meanwhile, we looked up for a suitable site for camping, but to no avail. Finally we located a cave to pass the night. A small tent was pitched for cooking our meals. There was a small spring thankfully available nearby for getting drinking water. Although the spring water collected in a small pond was shared by locals and their cattle as well, we managed to get dripping water collected in our bucket by placing a leaf near the source of the spring.

In the meanwhile, we had sent Karam Chand, our Tehsil peon, to Chichhe village, situated halfway to the lead mines, to arrange labourers for shifting our camp closer to the mines on the next day. Before the sunset, a strongly built hefty person approached us, accompanied by four gunmen. We got scared. However, when they reached our camp and greeted us with Jai Hind, we felt relieved. He introduced himself as the village head. We offered him a chair and some tea to drink. They left after a while with a promise to send about twenty guys to shift our camp to Chichhe village near the lead mines. The next day we shifted our camp and the day after started our regular mine survey work.

The work at Chichhe involved examination of lead mine pits, two or three in number. On the first day cleaning of the pit portals was carried out by removing the bushes and overgrown grass . The pits were slightly inclined.We threw burning cotton swabs soaked in kerosene into the pits to ward off wild animals sheltering inside. Suddenly groups of bats came out fluttering their wings. We waited in grim patience for any wild animals to come out, for about half an hour. To our great relief, there were none.Two labourers went inside the pit and cleaned the load surface. The same process was repeated for the next two pits.

In about a month, we completed our detailed survey around the lead mines. We shifted our camp, utilising the services of labourers from a local tribe known as the

Bakarwals. The Bakarwals are very sturdy people, but they do not carry baggage on their backs. It is done mostly on shoulders. The camp shift started early in the morning. Some labourers had reached the trolley bridge ahead of us and were resting, while others were following the tail end. When we reached closer to the bridge, I saw a naked labourer lying near a bush. His face was covered with his long Kurta. I instinctively thought that he was bitten by a snake. I went to him and tried to wake him up. He was startled and got up. Seeing that he is alive, I was relieved and asked him why he was not wearing his shalwars. He replied innocently that he had needed some padding to support the box he was carrying on his shoulder. Since he had reached first, he had rested and slept, covering his face with his kurta to ward off flies (without realising that he was naked).

We had organised the return trip much in the same way, as we had come by the trolley on the rope. The shifting operation took nearly the whole of the day and we could establish our camp at a village named Galar and start mapping the remaining area. After a while, we received a communication from the Srinagar Office that my senior colleague Mr Dhruva Rao had been promoted to the post of Superintending Geologist, hence he was to leave the camp immediately and proceed to the new place of posting, as per the Office Order. The communication to me also conveyed that Mr Rastogi would join my camp shortly.

❑

11

Encounter with a King Cobra

After Mr Dhruva Rao had left, I continued geological mapping from Camp Galar and awaited the arrival of Mr Rastogi. One day, I was taking a traverse through a granitic country, accompanied by two guide mazdoors. The terrain was full of boulders of granite rock with a lot of gaping joints. I was examining an outcrop and tried to measure the attitude of the rock joint with the help of a Brunton Compass. Just as I was about to hit the rock with my hammer to get a sample, I saw a snake crawling out of the joint. Its skin was mottled and perfectly matching with granitic rock. I got startled and held back my hammer. The guide mazdoors were shouting that there was a cobra in front of me and urged me to fall back quickly. I did so and asked them to stand still at their places.

It was the beginning of the warmer season and snakes came out of their hibernation and changed their skin at this time. The movement of the snake becomes sluggish, while they are getting their skin removed. Suddenly, the snake came out from the joint with its hood fully expanded, probably in response to sensing danger from us. There was a whitish loop on its head to indicate that it was a king cobra. I just remained standing, still holding the hammer in my hand. The guide mazdoors asked my permission to kill the snake, as it was highly poisonous. I forbade them to do any harm to the creature or make any movements. After a while, the snake closed its hood and sensing that there was no danger from us, left the scene swiftly. We were tense and felt relieved as soon as the snake had gone.

I told the mazdoors and a few passers by, who had gathered by that time, about the advantages of a snake. It keeps a check on the population of rats, which are so harmful to their crops. Moreover, it never harms unless one tries to disturb it or it feels potential danger from the human.

❑

12

On the Trail of a Bear

Himalayan bear is black in colour and has a white crescent below its neck. It is smaller in size as compared to the brown grizzly bear of Europe and North America. I was camping deep inside a forest, beyond Galar in Kishtwar area of the J. & K. State. I was taking a geological traverse across a nala (stream) section accompanied by three guide mazdoors. The undergrowth in the forest was negligible on the slopes. However, there was tall grass in the nala section and the guides were removing it with sickles to make it passable. Rock outcrops were scanty, but we examined in detail, wherever these were exposed.

I reached the nala bed by about noon. Suddenly, I noticed that the grass in the bed was depressed, as if somebody had been sleeping on it. The twigs were slowly unwinding. I was alarmed. There was a strong possibility that some wild animal had been resting on the grass and had left the place a short while ago. The guide mazdoors were of the same opinion and were more or less sure that it was a bear. They started looking for pug marks, which they found soon, and they were wet pug marks. The guides confirmed that it was a bear. I asked them to look for any smaller pug marks, as a bear with a cub is potentially dangerous.

We proceeded cautiously towards the other side of the nala slope, whistling and shouting. The excessive noise was necessary to ward off the wild animals, if they were in the vicinity. We kept on moving slowly, following the footprints. To our great relief, there were no footprints of a cub. We almost reached a ledge, where some rocks were exposed. I rested there and started examining the rock outcrop. The guide mazdoors were sceptical to go on the other side of the ledge, lest the bear was resting on the sunny slope. The bears often do this, to attack the enemy. However, the guides took due precaution by whistling and shouting and arming themselves with sticks and stones. They threw a couple of stone pebbles to ascertain if any animal was there. Finally they ventured onto the other side of the ledge. To their relief the bear was not there, although it had rested there, as indicated by the wet depressed grass in a hollow rock pit.

The bear seemed to have run down the forest slope to a patch of cultivated land, where corn crop was available for it to enjoy. I completed my traverse after examining a few rock outcrops on my return journey to the camp.

❑

13

A Pair of Bears with a Cub

Mr Rastogi joined me at the camp near Galar. After completing the work there, we shifted our camp upstream to cover the higher areas. The camp was located near the fringe of the forest at an altitude of about 11000 feet above mean sea level. We mapped the highest peak of the area from the camp, which was at about 14000 feet above mean sea level. We had started early in the morning and after successfully climbing to the top, we took another route to return back to the camp before the evening, without making any of the earlier mistakes.

Next day we went to cover the western ridge by geological mapping. We examined different rock outcrops till noon. It was a pleasant sunny day. Suddenly, we noticed a whole family of bears, mother, father and cub, basking in the sun just across the nala on the grassy knoll. Our guide mazdoor alerted us that this combination of bears with a cub was dangerous and we better leave. We observed the wind direction which was from west to east, i.e. from the bears towards us. We also observed the wild animals through binoculars. Apparently, they were not getting our smell through the wind as it was blowing in the opposite direction. We decided to sit there and have our lunch, while keeping a constant watch on the bears.

After finishing our lunch, it was decided to abandon the remaining part of the traverse, as it was not safe to proceed further. Moreover, it was already getting late for our return journey to the camp.

❑

14

Serious Injury

After about a week, we further shifted our camp to a location at a lower altitude. It was the middle of September and we had finished our work in the higher reaches. The plan was to cover the lower parts and gradually shift towards Kishtwar, which was the Tehsil (sub-division of a district) headquarter and was connected by a road to the Jammu-Srinagar highway.

In one of the traverses from the camp, we found a rock outcrop, showing a peculiar mineral assemblage. There were big crystals (porphyroblasts) of andalusite in a finer grained groundmass of chlorite and mica. Mr Rastogi was very excited. This rock indicated a higher grade of metamorphism in comparison to the garnetiferous mica schist seen so far. The rock was very hard and tough. He tried several hammer strokes to break off a sample for our laboratory studies, but it was of no avail. Suddenly, he hit the rock with great force. The hammer rebounded and pierced his left eye. Blood started gushing out. I took out my handkerchief and put it over the wound and fastened it tightly round his head. I asked one of the guide mazdoors to lift him on his back and take him back to the camp.

At the camp, I washed his wound with hot water mixed with a drop of Dettol and provided first aid with cotton and gauze bandages. A pain killer was given to him, as he was feeling severe pain by then. Mr Rastogi showed courage and perseverance and he was in full command of the situation. It was decided that he should be removed to Kishtwar, which was about twenty kilometres away, on a pony accompanied by the tehsil peon. I was to close the camp and follow him with camp equipment, shifting through head loads. Accordingly the pony and men were mobilised and Mr Rastogi left the camp by about 3:00 pm. Later, I learned that he had reached Kishtwar by midnight and had left for Jammu by bus the next morning, travelling a distance of about 200 km.

By the time I got the camp equipment packed and closed the camp, it was 4:00 pm. We hurriedly left the place with about fifteen labourers and the cook, Ghulam Ahmad Bhat. After travelling about half the distance, we managed to get a provisional shelter in a villager's hut at about 9:00 pm and called off for the day. A small tent was put up on the roof of the hut for me to rest there. The labourers managed to sleep within the hut, while the cook had organised his kitchen tent on the footpath itself. Next day morning, we resumed our journey by about 10 am, after having our breakfast and taking our packed lunch. Under such circumstances, Aloo parathas are the easiest to prepare and to serve for both the meals. We reached Kishtwar by about 3:00 pm, completely battered by the long journey and restless sleep during the night. The tehsil peon reported to me that Rastogi Sahib had left in the morning by bus to Jammu. He could get only scanty medical aid in the early morning, by way of some painkillers and vitamin tablets. We presumed that he must have reached Jammu that evening.

Soon we organised our camp at Kishtwar and reported about the mishap to our Superintending Geologist and also asked his permission to close camp for the current Field Season. A jeep with trailer and a pickup arrived by the end of September and I left for my headquarters at Jammu after closing the camp.

❑

15

Hill Diarrhoea

In the year 1968, I was to continue geological mapping in Upper Chenab Valley. Mr Om Prakash joined me in this task. We reached Kishtwar in the month of May '68. We collected our rations from the fair price shop on special permits. The ration was subsidised so that we got Jammu Basmati rice for Rupees 37 per quintal. A peon from *Tehsil* was deputed with our party to liaise with local people and help in shifting our camp. We decided to cover the northern part of the Chenab Valley first. This time, there was a rope bridge available over the Chenab River to cross to the northern side. Accordingly, we shifted our camp to a place near Dul village, by mules and started geological mapping from the point I had left in the last Field-Season. After about a week, we shifted our camp across Chenab River by head load through the rope bridge. Moving on a rope bridge was an experience of its own kind. One has to hold the two wire ropes by each hand and move carefully over the wire mesh below the feet. When one reached the middle, the whole rope bridge swung due to prevailing wind along the river channel. One has to keep composed, bold and maintain balance on the rope, at the same time keep moving cautiously over the wire mesh. Anyhow we managed to cross the bridge and establish the camp at a suitable place and resumed our work.

We carried out geological mapping of the lower reaches and moved to higher altitudes as summer was becoming hotter. Vegetables were scarcely available and our cook Ram Kishan had to choose between two types of vegetables: potato & onion and onion & potato. Fortunately, we two officers and Ram Kishan were non-vegetarians hence procuring chickens was Ram Kishan's responsibility, and he used to do very efficiently. One day, one of our guide mazdoors brought a leafy vegetable, locally known as *Karam*. He gave some to our cook. I did not like the vegetable much, but ate it as we got a green vegetable after a long time. Next day, my stomach got upset. It was because of the leafy vegetables or cold of the hill or both, I could not guess. I took some medicines but to no avail. Occasionally, I took curd or buttermilk during the day, as per its availability, but this too was not effective.

The diarrhoea continued for two weeks. I lost some weight and was feeling weak. I tried different combinations of medicines available with us, but loose motion continued unabated.

At the next camp, we got a guide with a double barrel gun. He was a local hunter and boasted about his exploits in scanty forest in an otherwise steeply sloped terrain. He came to know about my diarrhoea problem. He suggested that I should try mountain goat's meat, to get rid of the diarrhoea. His logic was that the ailment was due to exposure of the stomach to cold, which I might have done unwittingly at some time or the other. Since everything has failed, I decided to try this. He volunteered to go hunting for the mountain goat, locally called *Pijjhar.* This variety of goat runs very fast, particularly across scarps and steep slopes.

The guide reported to me for two consecutive days in the evening that he could not get the game for this reason or that. I told him that he was not a good hunter and that he was wasting our time. Next day early in the morning we heard a loud thud from a nearby *nala.* Soon he came to our camp along with his trophy, a dead *pljjhar* on his shoulders. He was not very happy with his success, as he usually never hunted while the animals gathered for drinking water. He said that hunting is a sport and he should shoot the animal providing him fair opportunity for his defence. I regretted my remarks made a couple of days back, but did not express the same before him. However, we enjoyed the meat cooked for dinner that evening. During the night both I and Mr Om Prakash felt rather warm in our sleeping bags. We had to open the zip of the sleeping bag to be comfortable. There was no loose motion the next day. On the contrary, there was no motion at all for the next couple of days. We continued eating pijjar*'s* meat for the next two days and I got rid of the chronic hill diarrhoea.

❑

16

The Thrill of First Flight

After completing field work along the Chenab Valley in October '68, Mr Om Prakash and I returned back to Kishtwar and camped in the campus of a temple close to the bus stop, at Kishtwar. We waited for vehicles for our return journey, but there was some problem in getting vehicles from Headquarters Srinagar. After a few days, we contacted a private bus operator for taking us to Srinagar along with our camp equipment and staff. The bus operator agreed to do so for a reasonable price and we packed off the next day to Srinagar, reaching there by evening. As the leader of the party, I reported to the Director, J. & K. Circle, the next day about our field work and the travails of our return journey, apprehending some adverse comments. The Director, Mr T. K. Kurien seemed satisfied and was rather happy that we saved Government money by engaging a private bus operator on a much cheaper cost. He, however, informed me that a seminar was being organised at the Regional Headquarters, Lucknow on 'Exploration and Development of Non-Ferrous Metals in India' in November '68 and instructed me to prepare a scientific paper immediately on my work carried out in Chichhe Lead Mines area with Mr B. K. Dhurva Rao in the previous Field-Season.

Before leaving on the field expedition, I had settled my wife and the newly born baby girl in a rented accommodation of a Kashmiri Pundit's house in Jawahar Nagar (Srinagar) with a household servant to support her daily chorus of work. The landlord had three or four young daughters, who gave good company to my wife and the child. However, the domestic servant left for his native place just after a couple of months, which caused inconvenience to my wife and concern to me. I attended these and other family matters within the next couple of days, before embarking on the next venture of writing a scientific paper for presentation in a seminar and later its publication in the Records of G.S.I. This was a novel experience for me therefore, I started consultations of such scientific papers in our meagre library of J. & K. Circle. Mr T. K. Kurien, the Director of the Circle, guided me and helped me immensely in this regard. Soon a draft paper was ready, though filling in different data tables and incorporating maps was still to be done. This was carried out in the next couple of weeks. Finally, a map which was incorporated in the paper was not found in our map section and they informed us that this was available in our Jammu

Office. A vehicle was leaving for Jammu the next day for some other errands. As the deadline for submission of paper was approaching, I was asked to proceed to Jammu with the same vehicle, get the map traced and return back to Srinagar immediately by taking a flight.

As a Junior Class One Officer, I was not entitled to travel by aeroplane. However, The Director has powers to grant such privilege under contingent circumstances. I left for Jammu the next day by road early in the morning and reached there by the evening. I managed to get the map traced the next day and booked my flight for the subsequent day. There was only one flight from Jammu to Srinagar by a small plane, Fokker Friendship, accommodating some thirty to forty passengers. The fare was Rs. 49 per person at that time, while the bus fare from Jammu to Srinagar was Rs. 15 and Rs. 24 for ordinary and deluxe class, respectively. The air ticket was booked from the Indian Airlines office located at the Tourist Reception Centre, Jammu. I was told to reach Jammu Airport one hour before the departure of flight for getting boarding pass and security checks, etc. The plane was to depart at 10:00 AM, however, I reached Jammu Airport located in the cantonment area of Satwari not far from my office in Gandhinagar, at 8:30 itself in my anxiety for not being late for the flight.

I was virtually the first to board the plane and was thrilled to see the sitting arrangement in the cabin. I was guided by the air hostess to my seat as per my boarding pass. She gave security instructions and asked us to fasten our seat belts. The plane started soon and was running on the runway increasing its speed constantly. Suddenly, with a slight jerk we were in the air. Being a geologist, I started watching the approaching foot hills, comprising Siwalik rocks of the Outer Himalaya. After a while, we entered the Lesser Himalayan Zone having rugged topography. The plane was constantly gaining height. After about fifteen minutes of flight we saw the Pir Panjal Range. Further on the Kashmir Valley was visible between Pir Panjal Range and the Central Himalayan Range. It was amazing to see the entire region, which I visualised till then through maps on piecemeal basis. After another ten minutes the plane started descending. We could see the snaking Jhelum River in the vast plain of Kashmir Valley. We were now approaching the runway and after a while, the plane touched the runway with a thud and slight jerk. I sighed a relief for being on the land again. We disembarked the plane in a queue and walked up to the small terminal building of Srinagar Airport.

After collecting my baggage, a small suitcase, I headed for the gate, where I was greeted by the driver of a GSI Jeep. I boarded the vehicle and in the next thirty minutes, I was at my home. I was very happy to join my family, though still in a trance and marvelling that how I was at Jammu about an hour back.

❑

17

First Paper Presentation in a Seminar

A 'Colloquium on Exploration and Development of Non-Ferrous Metals in India' was organised by the Northern Region of Geological Survey of India at Lucknow in November, 1968. I was asked by the Director J. & K. Circle, Mr T. K. Kurien to prepare a scientific paper on the occurrence of lead mineralisation in Chichhe area, where I had worked during the previous Field-Season (1966-67). I duly submitted the paper just in time and the same was accepted for presentation in the seminar. The Government Offices were shifted in early November from Srinagar to Jammu for winter and vice versa in summer, under the 'Darbar Move', a practice followed since the times of Maharaja Hari Singh. Accordingly, we shifted to Jammu with bag and baggage and settled in our old landlord's house as a tenant in early Nobember'68. The seminar was scheduled in the third week of November. I, along with my brief family, left for Lucknow by train to reach a day ahead of the seminar.

We were received at the Charbagh Railway Station of Lucknow by Mr C.P. Vohra, who headed the reception committee of the seminar. Mr Vohra, a mountaineer and a member of first successful team of Everest Expedition in 1965, was then posted in the J. K. Circle of GSI, where I had joined in 1966. I had met him when he visited the Circle later in 1966, after receiving a promotion and Padma Shri award for his feat. He offered the front seat of the vehicle to us and sat in the back. This gesture of concern for my wife carrying an infant baby by a senior officer filled me with gratitude and imprinted the laudable tradition of GSI officers in my mind permanently. We were dropped at our close relative's residence in Balda Colony across Gomti River, nor far from the Regional Office, located on Gokhale Marg.

The Inaugural Session of the seminar was held on the next day with due fan fair with lectures and presentations by the stalwarts like Muktinath, Shailesh Chakrawarti, A.P. Subramaniam and others, whom I did not know and saw them for the first time. The lunch break was enjoyable where I met and befriended some younger geologists. The afternoon session was organised in the auditorium of National Botanical Research Institute (NBRI) and was devoted to mineral occurrences of different localities with specific problems. I attended the session with a view to see and learn how the delegates are presenting their paper. In those days enlarged maps were displayed on the front wall where the author could explain his point or use the black board for elaborating further details. Manual slide projector was also available to a few who brought their black & white slides. There was a cultural programme organised using the talents of GSI and some local artists. My wife with her cousins (two younger sisters and a brother) attended the function and enjoyed the dinner which followed it.

My presentation of the paper was scheduled in the afternoon session of the next day. The organisers helped me in putting up two maps on the front wall before my presentation. I was a bit nervous but gathered courage from the fact that the audience was rather thin. Mr Shailesh Chakrawarti was in the chair with a co-chairman. I knew Mr Chakrawarti since my university days as he was then the Superintending Geologist of U.P. Circle and visited the Geology Department of Lucknow University on different occasions. I was soon invited to present my paper. I went to the stage confidently and reached the podium and greeted the chairman and the audience. I introduced the topic and the area confidently as I had mugged it up several timed during my preparations for the talk. While proceeding further, I was a little incoherent and so started reading from the paper without pausing and looking to the audience. I paused before the conclusion, as I was a bit more confident by then, and gave my concluding observations in a better manner. The paper was over within the stipulated time and was open to questions. I gave answers to some question but did not comprehend well the other questions. My Director Mr Kurien and the Chairman came to my rescue and intervened by elaborating the point on my behalf. Finally the Chairman Mr Chakrawarti thanked me and said few encouraging words about my painstaking field work in an inaccessible terrain and presenting the same in the seminar. He wished me well for my future endeavours.

After the presentation of my paper, I met my Director who was sitting in the front row. He shook my hands and congratulated me for my maiden effort. He, however, remarked that why I went like a mail train after my introduction of the topic. I told him frankly that I was a bit nervous and tried to finish the paper within the stipulated time. He liked my frankness.

❑

18

Visit of the Minister to Srinagar Office

Sri Ram Murti Ji, our Honourable Deputy Minister in the Ministry of Steel, Mines and Metals, Government of India, visited the Srinagar office in June '69. We had organised a welcome function for him in the lawn of 'Nilofar' building, where the office of J. & K. Circle, GSI was located. Mr T. K. Kurien was our Director and he had invited Mr V. K. S. Varadhan, his senior, who had come to the State Directorate of Geology and Mining (DGM) on deputation from GSI, for the welcome function. Sri Ram Murti Ji was a hefty person, occupying the central chair, flanked by the aforementioned directors. The welcome function went on smoothly with exchange of pleasantries and presentation of flower bouquet.

After tea and snacks, we officers, sitting in the front row, were introduced to the honourable minister. The Minister expressed satisfaction with the work we had been carrying out in the Circle. Suddenly he asked about the height of a poplar tree standing near the boundary wall of the Nilofar building. Our senior officers estimated it to be about 95 to 100 feet. Mr Kurien concurred with about 100 feet. In the meanwhile, Mr Varadhan made an angle of 45 degrees with his thumb and forefinger to coincide with the top and bottom of the tree. Then taking his hand far in the back for a distance of about metre and estimated an angle of 42 degrees with his thumb and forefinger such that he could sight the top and bottom of the tree. Then calculating the height by sextant method, he pronounced the height of the poplar tree to be 107 feet. The Honourable Minister was impressed with his surveying skill and was highly pleased. We also applauded Mr Varadhan for his acumen.

After the Minister had departed, we asked Varadhan Sahib as to how he could estimate an angle of 42 degrees with his thumb and forefinger. He smiled and said that the technique of surveying should not only be true but also be demonstrated to be true. We appreciated his presence of mind to handle such a delicate situation.

❑

19

Night with a Bakarwal Family

In the next Field-Season (1968-69), Mr Om Prakash was assigned to carry out geological mapping in Marau (*Marwa)* valley with me. We arrived at Kishtwar, the Tehsil headquarters, in the month of June' 69. After making necessary arrangements and acclimatising for a week, we crossed Chenab River through a wooden bridge, which connected Kishtwar with Ekhale and Sondar through a mule track. At Ekhale, we had the privilege of staying in a forest guest house, which was reasonably good. We finished the work around here by late June and decided to shift our camp to the next location in a *nala* section, having a few flat terraces. We hired the mules from nearby localities. The muletiers took time to reach our camp at Ekhale and assemble there. The muletiers always move in a group and therefore, the main column with camp equipment, etc. could only be dispatched in the afternoon with our cook Ram Kishan in the lead. He was duly instructed about the location of the camp, where he was to establish the camp and await our arrival. We were the last to leave after winding up the camp, along with the *tehsil peon* and a couple of guide mazdoors, carrying our essential commodities.

We moved at a fast pace, but the mules were faster. In their enthusiasm to reach the proposed campsite before night fall, the mules moved faster than usual and had crossed the *nala* section, where the camp was to be established. They moved to the next stream valley and off loaded the camp equipment, etc. at a suitable place. Ram Kishan soon got the tents pitched and started for the preparation of food. By the time we reached the proposed *nala* section, it was getting dark. The tents were not seen throughout this valley up and down. After a thorough search, whistling and shouting by the men with us, we concluded that the muletiers must have gone further and offloaded the mules. There was no use going further as the mules could not be loaded again on the same day and also, it was not safe to move in the dark in the thickly forested areas of Marwa valley.

The problem was where to stay for the night. The peon went around and looked for some habitation around. It was a desolate and forested area. After a while, he located a *Dera* (camp) of a Bakarwal's family by the bank of Marau River. Bakarwals are a nomadic tribe of the area. They move with their cattle - mostly goats, buffalos, ponies and ferocious watch dogs. The entire family moves during the summer months from the plains of Jammu area up the Himalayan hills, reaching to the Pir Panjal Range by September. As the higher reaches receive snow, they start moving down till they reach the plains by January. They start moving up again in March. The cycle goes on year after year. The marriages, childbirth and other rituals of life are performed during this to and fro journeys.

The tehsil peon approached them and narrated our plight. The head of the family came to us and offered that we stay with them. Since there was no alternative, we readily agreed to his invitation and went to his *Dera.* A fire was lit at a central place with blankets spread around it for our sitting. The peon and guide mazdoors made themselves comfortable on tarpaulins. After exchanging pleasantries and local news about here and there, the Bakarwal asked us for dinner. He brought two hot thick corn chapatis (locally called *doda*) with fresh butter in the form of a large big lump put on the chapatis. We ate one each, which was sufficient for us. The host was insisting on having one more, but we could not oblige him. The meal ended with a big glass of buttermilk, in place of water.

After the other guys finished their meals, we were escorted to a nearby hut of a *gujjar*, which was located in the middle of a corn field. The hut was inhabited during the summer months, mainly for keeping a watch over the corn crop. We were accommodated on the first floor of the hut to sleep on the rough blankets spread on the floor. Fortunately, we had our sleeping bags and air pillows. We slept comfortably during the night. Early next morning, we were awakened by a sensation of warmth on the head side. We came out of the sleeping bag to find that it was due to burning of wooden logs in a hearth and the woman of the house was preparing corn *dodas*.

We immediately got up and readied ourselves for locating our camp in the daylight. It was not difficult to find the tents in the next *nala* section with mules grazing fresh grass in the valley. Soon our camp was established at a suitable place to resume further work.

❑

20

Travails of Ram Kishan

The month of August '69 was full of turbulence and turmoil. In the beginning of the month, I received a telegram informing me that I have been blessed with a daughter on 24th July 69, almost at the same time when the whole world was anxiously watching the safe return of astronauts of NASA's first moon landing mission back on the earth. Later, we named her Apoli, after the Apollo-11 mission. She was born through a caesarean section and my wife was still in the hospital due to postnatal complications. This was the big cause of anxiety for me and more so because I was not able to go and see her, being the leader of the expedition party. The only solace for me was that my wife and the child were in good care of her parents.

In the meanwhile, Mr Om Prakash received a telegram about the serious illness of his father. He left Sondar camp that very day, marching the entire distance of about 35 km on foot. He reached Kishtwar the same day in the night and left for Jammu the next morning by bus. He could provide necessary medical attention to his father at Jammu. After his father's condition improved in about a week, Mr Om Prakash joined back the camp by the middle of August.

During this period, I had shifted part of my camp to a place at higher altitude, off Sondar, to complete mapping of that area. The contingency money was nearly exhausted and I was waiting for the recoupment from my headquarters at Srinagar. On his next trip to the post office at Kishtwar, our dak runner Maya Ram brought the intimation letter from the post office that the money has reached there by an insured parcel and I should collect it personally. As I was the only officer available, I could not leave the camp to go to Kishtwar to collect the money. Under the circumstances, I gave an authority letter to my office bearer cum cook, Ram Kishan, to collect the insured parcel and bring it to the camp. I waited for Ram Kishan's arrival on the due date and a day after, but in vain. Finally, I decided to close the subsidiary camp and come back to the base camp at Sondar. From there, I left for Kishtwar along with a search party, with a lurking fear whether Ram Kishan was waylaid for the money or had become prey to some wild animals, *en route.* We kept on inquiring about the whereabouts of Ram Kishan throughout our journey to Kishtwar but without any success or an adverse report.

On reaching Kishtwar the next afternoon, I went straight to the post office. There, I came to know that Ram Kishan had collected the insured parcel on the expected date under his proper signature. The Postmaster also told me that he opened the envelope and took his salary out of it and bragged that he was an assistant to Sahib and he is going to visit his family for a week. On his return only, he will join the camp and handover the money. I awaited his arrival at Kishtwar for nearly the whole week but it was of no avail. In the meanwhile, the matter was reported to the Director of J&K Circle and a police complaint was lodged against Ram Kishan for misappropriation of government funds and hampering the government work. The second instalment of contingency money reached me soon and I returned back to Sondar camp to resume further work.

I learnt subsequently that Ram Kishan had reported back at Srinagar office after about a fortnight, carrying the contingency money in an open envelope. He pleaded guilty for opening the envelope, on the pretext that his daughter was seriously sick. The office disbursed his salary, recovered the contingency money and suspended him for temporary misappropriation of government funds and unauthorised absence from duty. Since the matter was reported to the police, a case was instituted against Ram Kishan in the Kishtwar court. We were summoned by the court for recording our evidence in the month of January, when the area was under a couple of feet of snow. This was a novel experience for me and I was a bit nervous. The Administrative Officer accompanying me was a professional lawyer before joining G.S.I., hence he was a great source of strength to me. After my evidence was over, the magistrate was quite courteous to offer me a chair and allowed me to sit in the courtroom, which was kept warm by burning a *bukhari.*

The case lingered on for about two years. Finally, the court in its judgement exonerated Ram Kishan, accepting his plea that his daughter was critically sick and he was constrained to open the envelope containing government money to save his daughter, assuming that the envelope contained his salary also. The court allowed departmental proceedings for his unauthorised absence from duty. The office gave him serious warning for the lapse in his conduct and revoked the suspension. He got a substantial amount of money by way of his withheld salary for the period of suspension.

The positive outcome of this episode was that Ram Kishan became a sober person by reducing his alcohol intake, under my constant supervision and guidance. On my advice, he deposited the money in his savings account and also agreed to look for a suitable boy for his marriageable daughter. I left Jammu in April, 1972 on transfer to take up another assignment at Dehra Dun. However, I learned subsequently that he performed the marriage of his daughter with due festivities on a reasonably good scale.

❑

21

Bullfight on a Precipice

By the middle of September' 69, We had to shift to a subsidiary camp at Karai Pokkan, located in a remote area on the top of a precipice, overlooking the Marau River. We left the base camp, located at the other end of Sondar valley, along with four mazdoors carrying our essential camp equipment. Maya Ram accompanied us as the cook. We reached Karai Pokkan late in the afternoon. It was a small village comprising about five or six huts clustered together. The main occupation of the villagers was cattle raising, as no farmland was available in the vicinity. When we reached close to the village it was dusk time and the sheep, goats, cows and bulls belonging to the villagers were returning home after grazing in the nearby meadows.

There was a competition among the cattle for rushing home as it was getting dark and cold. Suddenly, two bulls started fighting to establish their supremacy over the herd of cows. The path was narrow and uneven. They locked their horns and pushed each other, initially mildly, but it became ferocious as the fight lingered on. The boys looking after the cattle herd were busy with some other errands and did not intervene till our guys shouted at them to look after the fighting bulls. By the time they reached the site and tried to separate the bulls, the stronger bull pushed the other one more ferociously towards the precipice. Finally, despite the intervention of the two boys, the stronger bull gave a jolt with great force, pushing the other bull down the precipice. The latter tumbled on the steep slope of the precipice and died instantaneously on reaching the base of the slope.

The women folk of the village started wailing and cursing on the loss of the bull. They also felt that our coming to the village was not a sign of good omen. They did not want our camp to be established there. This was a peculiar situation for us. I asked Maya Ram, who was a local resident, and the Tehsil Peon to talk to the villagers about our survey work and its importance for their development. Negotiations went on for a while. Ultimately, the villagers were convinced that no harm would come to them by our stay for a couple of days there. Moreover, we would provide employment to a few persons for those days and pay them at full government rate. They allowed us to pitch a small tent for our kitchen and provided a room for our stay.

We stayed there for three days and finished the survey work of the adjoining area. The village head came to see us off on the last day. He was highly appreciative of our sober behaviour and respect for the women of the village. He offered us a rooster as a parting gift. However, we insisted on payment for the same, which he accepted very hesitatingly. We felt very happy and satisfied to finish the survey work in a very remote and inhospitable terrain, with the cooperation of the villagers.

❑

22

Selfless Service of Maya Ram

It was September end and some areas at altitudes of about 12,000 feet, off Sondar in Marwa Valley, were still to be mapped. We, therefore, shifted to a subsidiary camp at an altitude of 10,000 feet, taking some guide mazdoors with essential camp equipment and Maya Ram as the cook. We planned for four day's work and, therefore, kept the rations accordingly including for one additional day, if need be. We carried out some work while going to the new campsite, which was located at the fringe of the forest overlooking a beautiful meadow. We settled there by the evening.

Next day, we took a geological traverse by climbing up to the ridge top. The weather became inclement in the evening and it rained intermittently throughout the next day. The clouds lifted the third day and we could do our job. It remained clear on the fourth day as well. However, it became foggy and overcast with clouds on the fifth day, so no work was possible and we remained confined to our tent. Fortunately, the sixth day was a good sunny day and we could finish the work by the late afternoon. Next day we decided to close our camp and move to the base camp taking another route so as to see some rock outcrops exposed in the forested area *en route*.

Maya Ram served us the breakfast of *Aloo Paratha*, as usual. After we had finished one *paratha*, he told me that there is no more flour available. I enquired about his meals, to which he hesitatingly told that he will have it on reaching the base camp. I reprimanded him that he should have told me this fact in the beginning itself, so that we all could have shared whatever meal was available. Maya Ram very humbly replied that our need was more important as we had to work on our return journey. I proposed to him to go to base camp by the shorter route, while we will manage with one guide mazdoor. He declined the offer on the plea that the area is forested having wild animals in it and it was advisable to go together. He was not prepared to leave us unsecured. I agreed with him and started our work. On reaching the last outcrop to be observed, I asked Maya Ram to proceed to the base camp along with two mazdoors and prepare food for us. We reached the base camp around 3:00 PM and had our lunch. So did Maya Ram. But his loyalty and self-sacrifice remained engraved in our memories.

❑

23

Reviving a Water Spring

I was to continue mapping in the Kishtwar area for the next Field-Season (1969-70). This time Mr B. K. Gupta was to accompany me in place of Mr Om Prakash. A resident of Jammu, Mr Gupta was an efficient manager. We arrived at Kishtwar by the middle of May '70 and organised the expedition party. Maya Ram also joined us in the meanwhile from his native place Sondar. The party left Kishtwar to establish the first camp across Marwa River, near Mughal Maidan.

No sooner did we establish our camp than a delegation of local villagers came to see us in the afternoon. They apprised us about a water spring in the nearby *nala*, which was no longer flowing. Consequently, they were hard pressed for potable water for themselves as well as the cattle of the village. I told them that we are not experts in Geohydrology, however, we will examine the area and let them know the possibility of reviving the water spring. They had brought some vegetables from their farms, as a token of their appreciation of our work in the area, which we graciously accepted.

Next day morning when we started our traverse, a team of villagers accompanied us to show the location of the spring. The position tallied well with the position already marked on the map. We observed the topography and geology of the area and measured the attitudes of the bedrock and joints. On our assurance that we will do further examination in a couple of days and will revert back to them, they went back and we resumed our work. We returned back to our camp in the afternoon that day. After our lunch and brief rest, we sat to plot data and summarise the day's observations, as per the routine practice. We noticed that a longitudinal river was flowing behind the ridge at a higher level than the line of springs located beyond the village spring. It looked plausible that the river water was feeding these springs through a set of joints. The direction also tallied well with the observed set of joints. We concluded that the feeder joint of the village spring must have clogged due to silting and/or some tectonic activity.

Next day, we examined the adjoining *nala* section and located a suitable place at its intersection with the joint set and asked the villagers to dig for a possible source of water.

After a couple of days, we moved to the next camp, as the work was over around this camp. Suddenly, we noticed that a group of villagers were approaching our camp, singing and dancing with a drum and carrying a goat. I thought it to be a local ritual procession. When they reached our camp, they jubilantly narrated the story of digging at the place indicated by us and they found copious water. As a thanksgiving, they had brought the goat for our consumption. We appreciated their gesture, but refused the offer on the plea that as Government Servant this was our duty to help people to the extent possible. They finally left our camp after profusely thanking us and leaving behind a rooster with our cook Maya Ram.

Word went around about this success story and every village in the locality, where we visited, wanted a water spring for them. The story of success snowballed into a common belief that we saw underground water through a machine and could predict its presence in the form of a water spring. In fact, the machine was only a radiometer through which we measured radioactivity of the rocks present in the area and it had nothing to do with locating groundwater. It was difficult to convince them that we are not experts of geohydrology and our work is different from locating water springs. Mr Gupta was hard pressed in explaining our position, in local dialect, to every other group approaching us for this favour. It was only after a couple of camp shifts that we got rid of this problem.

❑

24

Eye Drops

At one of the camps in Chhatru-Mughal Maidan area, a woman, with inflamed eyes, approached us for medicines. We gave her a few drops of Locula 10%, which we carried in our medicine chest for the use of the expedition party. In a couple of days, she was well, possibly due to the fact that the village folks in such remote areas do not have any access to modern medicines and her response was pretty good even with a mild dose of medicine. This encouraged other persons to come to our camp for medicines. We promptly asserted that we were not qualified doctors and suggested that they better go to the Primary Health Centre (PHC), located at Kishtwar, for their treatment. Maya Ram came to our rescue, as he hailed from the same region and could converse in the local dialect and convince them about the fact.

Most of the villagers were finally convinced and agreed to follow our advice to go to PHC Kishtwar for treatment of their ailments. However, a few young women persisted and wanted the eye drops for their inflamed eyes, which we obliged at the first instance. We, however, noticed that some of them wanted to have check-ups done by us for their genuine or imaginary troubles. They were loitering around the camp on some pretext or the other. We realised that providing them the medicines, even though in good faith, was not proper. Maya Ram had his own surmise that the women were of easy virtue. Whatever it be, we suggested they also consult a lady doctor at Kishtwar, and it was not appropriate to give medicines without proper check-ups.

We finished our work in the next couple of days and moved our camp to the next destination, located about 10 km from the place, not without learning a good lesson for the future about giving medicines.

❑

25

At the Base of Piparan Peak

In course of time, we shifted our camp at the base of Piparan peak, with a view to cover the area up to the top, which was located at an altitude of about 14000 feet. The camp had to be located close to the temporary hutments, as the only source of drinking water in the form of a spring was available in its vicinity. The temporary hutments, locally called *dera*, belonged to the villagers of Piparan, located a couple of kilometres down the slope. The men folk of the village were residing there itself, engaged in looking after the corn crop, which was maturing at that time; while the women folk shifted to the *dera* along with the cattle for grazing them in the meadows during summer months. Since the *dera* was occupied by the women only, they resisted our camping close to it. Mr Gupta somehow convinced them, speaking in local dialect, about the safe conduct of the inmates of the camp and also that there is no alternative source of drinking water in that locality. Finally, they agreed to establish our camp just above the *dera*, in prospect of some of them getting employment as guide mazdoors for the period we stayed there.

We took a traverse along the eastern ridge the next day accompanied by two women guide mazdoors. We used binoculars to look at the rock outcrops located at far distances. The women guide mazdoors were curious about the binoculars and wanted to have a look. I discouraged them from any such kind of distraction during our work, but promised to oblige them when we returned to the camp in the afternoon. I presumed that they would forget about the binocular, but they reported dutifully late in the afternoon along with a few more girls. All of them enjoyed looking through the binoculars. They were amazed to see some known spots located far away from the *dera* so near through the binoculars. Also they could perceive vivid details of the place. This went on every afternoon till the entire population of the *dera* had seen their places of interest.

Next day, we went to the Piparan peak. We left the camp rather early with a packed lunch. It was a gentle climb through meadows and ridges. Being late in the month of August, there was no snow at the top, except some snow beds in the shadow realms of the valleys. Plants were also scarce, except some juniper and birch trees. We reached the top by about 2:00 PM, perfect time for lunch. We enjoyed the pristine beauty as seen from the top; grassy meadows in the upper reaches followed by dense coniferous forest down below. We tried to locate Kishtwar and Doda towns, which looked like tiny clusters of human settlements. We safely returned to the camp by late afternoon through another route, examining outcrops exposed there.

After working for the next three or four days, we shifted our camp to the next location, on the way to Singpur Gali. The camp equipment was transported on head loads by men brought from the village down below. The women folk of the *dera* came out to bid farewell to us. Mr Gupta later told me that they said in their local dialect that they enjoyed our company and will be missing us.

❑

26

Camp Shift to Singpur Gali

Singpur Gali is a pass between Kishtwar area and the Kashmir Valley. Geological mapping was to be carried out up to Singpur Gali, in order to connect it with the map prepared from the valley side. It was the last week of September when we decided to shift our camp to Singpur. Labourers become scarce by the middle of September, as they get busy in collecting and stacking grass for their cattle to feed during the winter months. Our Tehsil peon had great difficulty in gathering sufficient labourers to shift the camp. However, he could muster the required strength of men by about noon and we started packing our camp equipment to proceed to the next camp. The route to Singpur was through a dense forest and the head of the column moved very fast to pass through the forest area before dark. We were at the tail end of the column supported by Mayaram along with two mazdoors, as usual.

By the time we reached the forested area, the evening was fast approaching. We took a path along the ridge and started descending. After a while, the path became insignificant. We tried to look for a footpath leading to the adjoining valley, but could not find any. Under the circumstances, we kept on moving down the ridge cautiously, while still looking for any path leading to the valley. On the contrary, the slopes on either side of the ridge became steeper. Suddenly, one of the mazdoors, carrying our kitchen box stumbled on a protruding rock and fell on the slope. I tried to save him, but could get hold of his rope only. The kitchen box tumbled down the slope. From the sound of the box when it reached the valley floor, we could estimate that the fall must have been to the tune of 200 feet. The mazdoor was dangling from the rock ledge, while I was holding the rope and shouting for help. Mr Gupta, Maya Ram and the other mazdoor rushed to rescue the guy. With some effort, we could finally bring back the mazdoor on the ridge. Fortunately, he had only suffered light injuries and felt some relief after we provided him with first aid. It was dark already, so we looked for a flatter place on the ridge and decided to pass the night under the open sky. We gathered enough wood, twigs and leaves, and started a bonfire, which kept on burning throughout the night to ward off wild animals present in the forest. We had our dinner of Aloo paratha, which Maya Ram had kept separately. We spread a tarpaulin on the ground and zipped inside our sleeping bags. Maya Ram and the labourers managed with few blankets, as they were on guard duty alternatively.

Next day, we got up very early due to the morning chill breeze. At the daybreak, I along with Maya Ram and a labourer, proceeded down the valley towards Singpur village, where the head of the column was supposed to have reached. Mr Gupta with the other labourer meticulously searched the slope to locate the contents of the kitchen box scattered all over. It was Mr Gupta's calibre that he could locate the pressure cooker weight and stove pins, so critically essential for cooking.

After walking for a couple of hours, I saw the camp of the Atomic Energy Commission, close to the Singpur village. To our pleasant surprise, our labourers with camp equipment were stationed there only. The Geologist of AEC, Mr Nikam greeted us. He told me that they were about to send a search party for us. Mr Gupta joined us soon after for a sumptuous breakfast hosted by Mr Nikam.

The camp shift to Singpur was memorable to us for an entirely different reason. We had discovered Palaeozoic fossils from the shales close to Singpur Gali, when we took a traverse the next day.

❑

27

Maya Ram's Journey to Pathankot to See a Train

After completing the work pertaining to the Field Season 1969-70, in Chatru-Mughal Maidan- Singpur area, We reached Kishtwar, the *Tehsil* Headquarters, in the first week of October 70. It takes about a week to wind up the camp. This included asking permission to close camp and requisitioning vehicles for transportation of camp equipment back to the Headquarters; drying and packing of tents and putting them in proper gunny bags with labels written on them to be able to get them back from the Stores for next year's use, and completing official formalities at the *Tehsil* Office. Maya Ram was very curious to see a railway train.

In those remote areas, nobody has seen a train. Since I had to go to Lucknow, our Northern Region Headquarters, for getting the fossils, collected from Singpur Gali, identified in the Palaeontological Laboratory. I asked Maya Ram to come with me up to Pathankot Railhead. He readily agreed and came with us to Jammu.

Maya Ram stayed with Mr Gupta in Purani Mandi area of Jammu to procure grocery and other household utility items for his native village. In about a week's time necessary arrangements were made for my journey by train to Lucknow along with the fossil samples. On the appointed date, I along with Maya Ram left Jammu in the afternoon by a jeep for Pathankot. We reached there by 5:00 PM. Sealdah-Pathankot Express was a prestigious train in those days. It was standing on Platform No. 1. I had a first class ticket and so boarded the bogey just in front of the main gate. Maya Ram and the driver assisted in bringing the luggage to the first class coupe. Maya Ram was thrilled to see the train. He saw the bathrooms and the pantry car. After I was seated in the coupe, he, under the guidance of the driver, saw the train from the engine to the guard's compartment in the rear. He also saw the second and third class compartments and enquired about their fares. He finally came back to my compartment to say goodbye as the train was to leave in another five minutes. He was still wondering how all these houses (train compartments) move together on the rails. It must be pretty dangerous to keep the balance, while the train is running with speed.

I asked my driver to take back Maya Ram to Mr Gupta at Jammu. Next day he boarded a bus to Kishtwar. From there, he must have marched on foot to reach his home in Sondar village in two days. The stories about the train must have been equally thrilling to his village folks, who must have gathered around the fireplace to listen to him for quite some time.

❑

28

Leap of a Tiger

In the year 1972, I was deputed to Indian Photo-interpretation Institute (now IIRS) at Dehra Dun for studying aerial photo-interpretation. The course lasted for one year and included field checks in the Garhwal Syncline area during November '72. I along with Prof. R. P. Sharma and another officer co-trainee, reached Forest Rest House at Sindikhal late in the evening. The rest house is located off Dugadda on Kotdwar - Lansdowne road, well within the thick forest of Jim Corbett (now Raja Ji) National Park. An office peon, Khushal Singh, who hailed from Garhwal and was familiar to these areas, was deputed to accompany us for facilitating our work in the field.

After settling down at the camp, we took a geological traverse the next day from Dugadda to Hathi Danda, located in a tributary valley of Ramganga River. We moved along an un-metalled motorable road for about two kilometres. From this point onward the traverse was to be made on foot. So, we instructed our driver to take the vehicle back to Sindikhal camp and meet us on the road opposite Hathi Danda at about 5:00 PM. We must have gone for about 200 metres to examine a rock outcrop, when suddenly a tiger leapt across our path. All of us stood there stunned. Khushal Singh also gestured to stand still and keep silent. After about a couple of minutes, all six of us started shouting and whistling loudly, to ward off any possible companion of the tiger. Now we had to decide about our further movement, as we still had to cover a long way to Hathi Danda. After shouting for a while, Khushal Singh and the two local guides surmised that there are no other wild animals in the vicinity and hence we could resume our work.

After about another kilometre, the footpath ended near a limestone scarp. We had to examine the entire cross section of the rock exposed there. Hence, we started moving down the scarp cautiously. It was a difficult proposition, but there was no alternative. We had to hold the creepers where available and sometimes moving on all fours, clinging to the rock face. We examined some outcrops of our interest *en route*. The process continued for the next couple of hours till we reached a relatively flatter spot. We were exhausted by then and therefore stopped for lunch break and rest.

We resumed our journey down the scarp, examining the rock outcrops and negotiating the steep slope through zigzag joints and goat tracks. We reached the river bed by about 4:00 PM only to find tall grass grown all over. All of us started shouting and whistling once more to ensure the absence of any wild animal. This habitat was perfect for elephants - tall grass, lots of flowing water and wide flat river bed. We now realised how appropriate was the name of the place as Hathi Danda (meaning the abode of elephants). We cautiously moved along the river bed till we reached an open area. Here the river channel started braiding and it was possible to ford it. We started crossing the individual braid of the channels. Some were knee deep water, while others were deeper. It was getting dark and we wanted to cross the main channel of the river while it was still visible. With great difficulty we accomplished the job, thanks to the able guidance of Khushal Singh and the local guides.

When we reached the other side of the river, we noticed a fire lit on clear ground and was left burning. Khushal Singh told us that our vehicle had come there around sunset time, stayed there for a while and lit the fire in a manner that it kept burning for some time afterwards. This was a regular practice in the Survey of India, under such circumstances. He advised us to wait for a while as they make a second trip in a couple of hours. Soon we were on the road and located a dera of Gaddi tribe, whose main occupation was rearing sheep. We stayed at the dera for some time and were offered tea by the headman which we graciously accepted, as it was very much needed at the end of the day. Around 8:30 PM, the vehicle appeared on the road. Khushal Singh and the local guides rushed to stop it by waving their hands. The driver could spot Khushal Singh and stopped the vehicle. We boarded the vehicle and reached Sindikhal camp in the next half an hour, with dramatic narrations by Khushal Singh to the driver about the tiger's leap, our negotiating the scarp face, danger of elephants in the tall grass and fording the river at the dusk.

❑

29

Traversing through a Synclinal Closure off Rathwadhab

In early December, 1973, I was to carry out fieldwork in Rathwadhab area in Garhwal Himalaya along with two officer trainees of 1973-74 batch of Indian Photo-interpretation Institute (IPI), Dehra Dun, where I was working as Professor (Research). The party comprising Mr L. S. Suryanarayana, Mr H. N. Shukla and myself left Dehra Dun in a Land rover on a bright winter morning. We reached the forest rest house at Rathwadhab by the same evening and settled down.

We started our geological traverses from the next day onwards around Rathwdhab. After a few days we were to field check across the synclinal closure, which lay near a tributary stream joining Ram Ganga River. We went up to the stream on the vehicle and crossed over the stream through a foot bridge. I asked the driver to take back the vehicle and meet us in the evening on the other side of the mountain near a specific village. We moved along a *nala* section upstream to examine the rock outcrops exposed along it. Our journey was smooth up to the next couple of kilometres, till we reached a limestone scarp some 250 metres of sheer rise.

We examined the rock outcrop there, then started looking out for the way up. We saw a canal above the limestone scarp. That meant that the slope is gentler further up. We asked the local guide if there was an alternative route for going up. He suggested that we may go back to the foot bridge and take another route to the village located above the scarp. Since the time was running out, it was not advisable to go down and take the alternative route. Ultimately, we decided to negotiate the scarp somehow and reach up to the village. There was a bridle path on one side of the scarp, which went up to a certain distance. I asked the other two officer trainees to wait for me, till I went up and explored the path. I started moving cautiously along the bridle path, which became narrower as I moved upwards. The path ended at one point, where a shear joint met it in an oblique direction. I asked the two trainees to come up in a single file along the path and join me. They were a bit scared but made it to the point where I was standing. I again started moving up along the joint, holding the scarp surface by hand to have better grip. I reached a point where I could stand firmly on my legs. I asked them to follow me and reach up to that point. The progress was slow, though safe so far. Now the last leg of the journey was to be negotiated, as the small canal was visible. I asked our companions not to look downwards, lest they have the effect of vertigo. About 50 metres of scarp lay in front of us. I myself was a bit scared, but could not express it. I encouraged my friends that it was a small scarp and we have nearly made it. I led the way, using all fours, climbing upwards step by step. There were cross joints in the limestone, which facilitated my rock climbing. After gruelling for about half an hour, I could make it to the top and I laid there completely exhausted. After a while, I asked my friends to come up one by one, using the footsteps located by me and holding the rock joints. Fortunately, they also reached the top. We drank fresh water from the canal and regained our strength after resting for a while.

It was evening, when we finished our measurements and examination of the outcrop. We hurriedly moved along the canal on an even contour till we reached a pass. The village lay on the other side of the pass. Soon we reached there after crossing the pass. It was getting dark, however, we reached the mule path which connected the village to the road, a kilometre down below. We saw the fire put up by our driver and peon to indicate their presence. After another half an hour, we reached the road side and drove to Rathwadhab camp, where a lavish non-vegetarian dinner was waiting for us, courtesy our cook Khushal Singh.

❑

30

Field Work in the Teruel Province of Spain

I went to The Netherlands on a fellowship to pursue a Master's degree in Remote Sensing Applications in Geology at the International Institute of Aerial Surveys and Earth Sciences (ITC) based at Enschede. As a part of my thesis for the aforementioned M. Sc. degree, aerial photographs, covering part of Teruel Province of Spain, were to be studied and a geological map of the area was to be prepared. This required field checks around the villages of Villarluengo and Pitarke. Accordingly, my colleague in GSI and class fellow at ITC, Mr S. N. Mitra and I left Enschede with our Instructor, Mr Kovach in May '74 for Spain by road. The town of Enschede is located in the eastern part of The Netherlands, close to the German border. We left Enschede by car to Delft, near Amsterdam, to collect survey equipment, as it was the seat of the original ITC and some courses were still conducted there. We stayed there for the night and left early in the morning for Spain. We bypassed the capital cities of Brussels and Paris and reached a roadside chateau in the evening for our dinner and night stay. Next day we left early to cross the Alps by noon and entered Spain via Andorra. Finally we reached our destination, the village Pitarke located south of the town of Villarluengo.

Pitarke was a small village having about twenty houses on either side of the road. Bar Conchita, where we stayed as a paying guest, was located at the beginning of the village and was owned by a Spanish gentleman. He had two daughters, the bar was named after the elder daughter. The villagers were engaged in horticulture, forestry, fish (trout) farming and agriculture farming and had mules for the purpose. The nearest fish farm 'pici factoria' was at La Trucha (the Trout, in English). The houses were generally two to three stories, white painted from outside and decorated with blooming flower vases on the outer wall. During the summer months the days were longer, hence we could carry out field work for almost ten hours; leaving the camp after breakfast at 8:00 AM and and back by 6 to 7 PM, in time for the dinner. We used to carry sandwiches for lunch, which we ate at some coffee shop or road side bar, if available. The locals were always curious about the work we were doing. In order to communicate with them, I had a language translation book, which gave the most common sentences in all the main European languages. It was, therefore, possible to satisfy their curiosity, as well as, manage my requirements from the bar or coffee shop.

Our work started picking up soon. Mr Kovach had planned the traverses in such a manner that he will drop one of us at some point on the road and ask to meet him at another point after completing the traverse to be picked by him on his way back. In this manner we were able to field check our respective areas, which were located in the adjoining topographical sheets. One day, I finished my work early and reached the given point on the road, sitting on a rock piece, awaiting to be picked up by Mr. Kovach and Mr Mitra. I rested there for about half an hour. Suddenly, I saw a spanish person on horseback with guns, approaching towards me. I had heard about some terrorist activity in the forest areas of Ibero River Basin and was cautioned by my host about the presence of '*terroristo*' in these areas. I got a bit scared. Nevertheless, I got up and started waving my map and explaining him about the geological mapping ('carto geologio e minero'), in my broken Spanish. When he came near enough, I further elaborated that I am an International student of ITC, The Netherlands, etc. He was equally apprehensive about me. After alighting from the horse, he started telling me in broken English that he was visiting his forest and he resided at a locality at the base of the mountain, which was visible from the road bend. After a brief enquiries about each other, he mounted his horse and bid 'adios'. After another ten minutes, Mr Kovach along with Mr Mitra came in his car to pick me up for our camp at Pitarke. To the relief of everybody, I narrated my story of meeting a *'terroristo'* at the end of my traverse. Our host and the housemates at Pitarke equally enjoyed the story at the dinner.

A couple of days later, my host inquired about our traverse in a particular area, where his forest lay, as he wanted to go there to trim the branches of the trees. I said that we are going in that direction the day after. The next day, the two daughters were very upset with me. After some conversation, I could make out that their father is also taking them along with him for chopping off the branches. Had I not told them about our traverse on that side, they would have escaped this labour under the hot sun. I kidded them that this way they will get good sun tan, but the idea did not appeal to them. The next day all three of them proceeded with us to the forest *en route* to our field work. We came back late in the afternoon to pick them up for Pitarke. Our host was very happy that they could finish the forest job on time. He thanked us profusely, much to the chagrin of the daughters. However, to please the daughters, Mr Kovach promised to take them to the town of Villarluengo for an evening's outing on the weekend.

A couple of weeks later, a letter from my wife from India reached the Bar Konchita address. The daughters had, by now, known the name of my wife, hence they kept the letter in their safe custody till I returned back from my field work. They told me that a letter from 'signorita Usha' had come, but they would give me only when I treated both of them with a bear each. I promptly agreed as I was anxious to see the letter. We had a beer in the bar and I got the letter. Fortunately, everything was fine at home.

On another day, a bowl of soup was served to us before dinner. This was the usual practice, but the soup appeared slightly different, though tasty. After having a few sips Mr Mitra pointed out that some shells were seen within it. We both could not take it further, once having come to know that it was shell soup. On another occasion, a sweetened fruit salad was served as a sweet dish. This was called 'punche' in Spanish. I was fond of fruit salad hence had second helping. Soon, I felt dizzy. I asked my host as to how the dish had been prepared. He said that it had 'koniak' (a strong brandy 'cognac') as one of its ingredients. I was not used to taking alcoholic drinks hence, got totally intoxicated. I was taken to my bed upstairs, helped by the inmates of the house. I recovered the next morning fully fit and fine to resume our field work.

❑

31

Professor's Visit

Our Professor, Mr H. E. C. Van der Meer Mohr, was to visit us in the first week of June, 1974 to see our work and also to participate in the field checks for a NASA project on SKYLAB pictures covering Ibero River Basin, assigned to me as part of my thesis. Prof. Meer Mohr was a very focussed and meticulous person and a bit short tempered; any distraction in his plan or programme would irritate him. Hence, we were very cautious and under awe while working with him. The next day, we all accompanied him in his car. I sat in the front seat by his side with a map open on my lap, to guide him along the route and to stop wherever he wished to examine the rocks himself.

We had moved along the road for a good distance, suddenly he stopped and told me to examine the rock outcrop exposed on the other side of the road and it needed a u-turn to reach the spot. He gave a proper signal before making the turn. In the meanwhile a car approached towards us and the driver blew the horn. It was enough to upset Prof. Meer Mohr. He had perfectly made the u-turn and stopped the vehicle. He turned red in the face and I heard him muttering 'that impatient idiot, why should he blow the horn, when I am giving enough space for him to go !'. After a while, he moved to the spot, and it was business as usual.

On another day, we carried out our work successfully and stopped for our lunch by the side of a rivulet under the shadow of a few olive trees. We had sausage sandwiches, which Prof. Meer Mohr was eating with onions and garlic. He told us that he relished them and more so because he could not eat onions and garlic back home in The Netherlands, as nobody liked the smell, especially his wife. We rested for a while after lunch in the balmy air of Northern Spain, but had to move on as a lot of work was still to be done in the afternoon. We drove on till we reached a plateau area covered with pine trees. He took the car to a pine grove on the side of the road and fell asleep on the steering wheel. We quietly moved out of the car, without disturbing the deep slumber of Prof. Meer Mohr. When we settled below the pine trees, Mr Kovach told us that the Professor should not be disturbed till he woke up himself. After a nap of ten minutes, Prof. Meer Mohr called us, apologised and he was alert as usual for the work.

Next day we went towards Jaka town, which was pronounced as 'haka'. On our way back, he enquired about how we spend our weekends here. I told him that mostly we rest or sleep or go to Villarluengo, the nearest town. He suggested that we could visit a good bar located at La Trucha to get rid of our loneliness.

Our last day's traverse was rather short and we finished the work early in the afternoon. Prof. Meer Mohr asked me about the location of the point to be examined. I showed him the location on the map. After examining for a while, he suddenly remarked 'who has made you a Geologist?. I was shocked, thinking that I must have made some grave mistake while interpreting the geology of the area. After a short pause, he further added 'You should have been a Navigator, Oh my God! Not a single mistake in locating the observation points.' I was greatly relieved and was very happy at the Professor's remarks. I told him that location is the first thing that is taught in the GSI Training Institute.

On the conclusion of his visit, Prof. Meer Mohr offered to take us up to Zaragoza on the way to Madrid. The programme was that Mr Mitra and I would visit Madrid and a couple of other places on our return journey to The Netherlands, while Mr Kovach preferred to go directly by road. We were a bit hesitant in leaving the field a day earlier than the schedule provided by the ITC. Prof. Meer Mohr allayed our fears by telling that once we have completed our work, we are free to go anywhere and there will be no problem from ITC side. So, we happily accompanied Prof. Meer Mohr up to Zaragoza and took a train to Madrid.

❑

32

An Episode in Rome

Mr Mitra and I left Madrid by train to Venice and then to Florence. We stayed in Florence (Firenze, in Italian) for a day to see the picturesque city full of fresco and mural paintings and marble statues in beautifully laid gardens. The bridge on river Arno was fascinating, as it housed curio shops on either side. We went to Pisa the next day and then to Rome (Roma), reaching there in the evening. We stayed there for a couple of days and saw places of historical importance including Vatican City.

On the last day in Rome, we wanted to see the Colosseum and other monuments. We were moving on the footpath, discussing something about our field work in Spain. A person dressed normally said Hi and introduced us as a geologist working in Argentina. We were glad to see him and chatted with him for a while. We asked him about his geological experiences in Argentina. He immediately offered to go to a nearby restaurant for drinks. We graciously accepted the offer and accompanied him to the restaurant. He kept on discussing touristic spots to be seen in Rome and around, but avoided talking about the geology of Argentina. In the meanwhile a couple of girls of easy virtue appeared on the scene and joined us. We were a bit alarmed, therefore, after finishing our drinks quickly, we asked his leave, as we were to see places in Rome. He asked for the bill, which was exorbitantly high for the light drinks and some snacks we had. He faked to be cheated by the restaurant and appeared thoroughly perplexed. We suggested that he see the manager of the restaurant, but he told us that we all are duped and it was better we quietly pay the bill and get off before bouncers catch us and frisks us for all the money we had. He took out some money from his pocket and asked us to supplement for the rest from our side. Mitra had some travellers' cheques, while I had some hard cash, which we all pooled to pay the bill. Suddenly, an idea came to my mind; I requested the manager to either give us some money or get us dropped at our hotel. He preferred to get rid of us quickly and preferred to pay us back some money for our return journey, lest we report the matter to the police.

We came out of the restaurant and bid goodbye to the 'gentleman' from Argentina, who quietly went in the other direction possibly to seek for his new victims. We were a bit scared and felt disgusted at being duped like fools. The first thing we checked was for our cameras, which we tried to hide behind our jackets and also the passports we had kept in our under pockets. On finding these articles intact, we felt somewhat relieved. We decided not to visit any of the places planned for the day, instead we walked back to our hotel on foot, looking back every now and then, lest somebody is following us. We had some money left in our bags in the hotel, therefore, after the initial shock was over, we had a scanty lunch and slept in our room. We checked out of our hotel in the evening to catch the train from Rome to Zurich (in Switzerland).

❑

33

Cat in a Paris Hotel

My wife joined me in The Netherlands by the end of June '74. I was busy at ITC in post-field interpretation of the Montalban area of Spain I had visited recently. She developed fever due perhaps to severe change in climate, from the hot summer of India to the rather cold climate of Enschede. She was fine in a couple of days, thanks to the ITC Hotel dispensary and ever smiling nurse, Ms Grootenboer, who was impressed with my wife's dark tan and considered her beautiful. In the following week, my wife and I visited local tourist places one by one, by walking in the evening. Since the days were longer, we could stay out till 8:00 pm. On one such trip, her sandal's heel got detached. It was impossible for her to walk barefoot so I looked for some help around. She walked somehow for some distance till I saw a house with lights on. I pressed the doorbell of the house and a gentleman came out. I profusely apologised and narrated the problem. He was kind enough to take us to his garage and fixed the problem. We thanked him and left the place quickly as it was getting dark.

We planned a trip in middle July to Paris. I discussed the plan at the reception desk with Irene, a very helpful girl and requested her to help for our stay in Paris at a suitable hotel. In those days one could talk across Europe on a normal telephone call. There was no need for trunk dialling even to different countries of Europe. Therefore she, using her resources, booked a moderate suite in a hotel at Republic in Paris which was owned by an Indian. We left Enschede on the weekend by train and reached Brussels in the morning. We visited Brussels, Waterloo and Antwerp during the day and boarded a night train for Paris and reached there the next morning.

The metro trains at Paris are very systematic and user friendly. The information is given in French but also indicated with appropriate signs. So with our elementary knowledge of French, we could manage to reach Republic Metro Station easily. The hotel was not far from the station, hence we walked there with our meagre luggage. The manager of the hotel welcomed us and showed us our suite. We settled down in the room and were preparing to leave for the day's itinerary of visiting places of tourist interest in Paris. Suddenly my wife noticed a beautiful statue of a cat on the cornice of the fireplace. This fascinated her very much and she wanted to touch and caress it. No sooner did she approach the statue, it ran out of room with a sweet *meaau*. She was startled and was taken aback with slight nervousness. We left the room for our visit, wondering all the while how the cat could manage to enter the room.

❑

34

Menace of Honey Bees

In May, 1976 a committee was formed by GSI to investigate a reported fossil find from Dugadda, located near Lansdowne (now in Uttara Khand). The committee was headed by Mr B. N. Raina, Director Himalayan Geology Division, Mr P. C. Mehrotra, a senior Geologist of Palaeontology Division and I from Photogeology and Remote Sensing Division. I was specially included in view of my finding of Fenestella (Bryozoa) fossil from the same locality. We visited the area in June that year and examined the reported fossil locality in detail. Mr Raina left after a couple of days, while Mr Mehrotra and I continued with some field work in a related area around Satpuli, off Kotdwar.

In order to examine the entire sequence and its extension, we left Satpuli camp rather early in the day along Nayar River till we reached a tributary stream cutting across the structure. We left our vehicle and took a traverse on foot to examine the rock exposures. After finishing our work, we returned back to the point where we had left our vehicle and had a quiet and meagre lunch.

We left the place around 2 pm. We had hardly gone for a kilometre, then we noticed somebody shouting for help. The man was half naked making frenzy gestures and carrying a big fish tied in his pyjamas. We stopped the vehicle and asked the driver to enquire about the matter. We also got down to hear his story. The man narrated that he saw a big fish in a side pool of the Nayar River and tried to catch the same. After some efforts he had succeeded in his venture. Since the fish was too big to carry by hand, he tied the same in his pyjamas and carried it on his shoulder. Suddenly a cluster of honey bees appeared from a nearby tree and attacked him. Apparently the bees were disturbed due to his marathon fishing activity. He left his booty and ran helter skelter for safety, but it was of little avail. The bees stung him all over. Finally he rolled himself on the ground and laid in a semi-conscious state for a while. The cluster of bees left him after completing their mission. After a while, noticing that the danger was over, he limped and collected the fish and started moving toward Satpuli.

He requested for some petrol from the jeep to rub on the bitten spots on his body to alleviate his pain. We obliged him. It was a surprise to see that he got instant relief from pain and appeared more composed. He requested for a lift up to Satpuli, where possibly he used to sell fish. On alighting from the vehicle, he cut a sizable piece of fish and gave it to our driver as a goodwill gesture. He accepted the gift and gave it to our mess. We all profusely enjoyed the dish from fresh fish in our dinner that evening. It remained a topic of discussion among the mess guys and the driver for several days.

❑

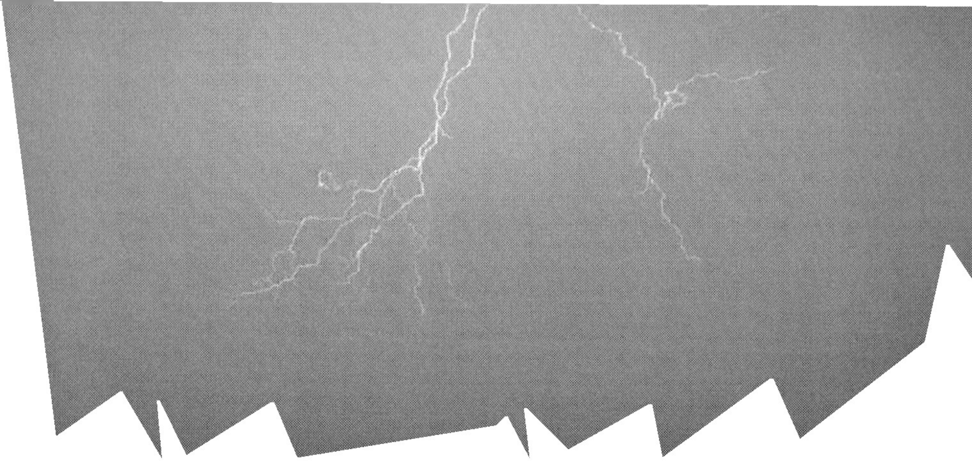

35

Caught up in a Storm

A week after the above episode we closed our camp at Satpuli and left for Luckinow by road. It was the end of June and the monsoon had set in, rather late that year (1976). We left Satpuli around 9 am after a heavy breakfast. It took some time negotiating the mountainous road up to Kotdwar. Once we reached Bijnor, we caught up to speed on the plain road. We thought of reaching Lucknow by late evening and hence did not waste our time for lunch. We stopped for tea at a dhaba along the road. Just before the town of Maholi, the driver informed me that there was no petrol in the tank. The petrol in the jeep had either leaked or had gotten depleted through some manual interference in connivance of the driver.

The driver requested many passing vehicles for petrol, but to no avail. I asked the driver to get a lift in one of the vehicles and buy petrol from Maholi. He boarded a truck and after about an hour came back with a can of five litres of petrol. We thanked our stars and resumed the journey. After a while dark clouds appeared on the horizon and with a gusty wind it started raining. Soon the intensity turned into a thunderous storm with lightning. The trees on the roadside started wallowing dangerously, often falling here and there. We cautiously continued our journey. After about an hour the storm stopped. The evening was fast approaching. We had to stop at a few places to skillfully negotiate and clear the road of the fallen trees. Sitapur town was not far away, when the vehicle suddenly stopped for lack of petrol. We had consumed the petrol while moving in low gears during the storm. It was dark and the place was desolate. The sound of insects was in an intense chorus after the first rain. We sat in the vehicle in stunning silence for some time. There was no way except looking for some passing vehicles, which were now less frequent. After a while the driver managed to get a lift in one of the trucks for fetching petro from Sitapur.

Once the driver had gone, I was the sole occupant of the vehicle. I moved out of the vehicle to see if some house or tea shop was around. There were none. Then I saw a flickering of light on the other side of the road, though a little far away. I was hesitant to explore. However, since I had to wait for the driver to come, I thought of going across the road and moved towards the house from where the light was coming. After walking for some distance I reached the spot. There was no house and it was a Mazar of a buried muslim sufi saint. The devotee there must have lighted the earthen oil lamp, after the storm had subsided and left for his night stay. I shouted 'Koi hai', but there was no response. I was a bit scared. Composing myself a bit, I went near the mazar. There were flowers and coins on the sheet covering the mazar. I bowed in reverence and stood there for a while. By this time, I was more confident and after staying for sometime, I left the place and moved towards my vehicle. I waited in the desolate dark place for some more time till the driver appeared in a vehicle fetching five litres of petrol again in the can. We left the place, passing by the mazar after saluting once again. In the meanwhile, I had narrated the whole story of the mazar to the driver. He was also full of reverence and bowed near the mazar and paid some coins in gratitude.

❑

36

Field Check in Sahibi Basin of Haryana

In the last week of September '76, there were excessive rains in Delhi and adjoining areas of Haryana. Large parts of Sahibi River Basin, in Gurgaon District, were inundated and the water stayed in the area for a long time, possibly due to poor drainage. Consequently, the crops of the area got damaged and the farmers of the area started agitating, demanding compensation and relief. The Haryana Government, in turn, approached the Central Government to come to their rescue. The Central Government extended help to the extent possible, but thought of finding a permanent solution to the problem, in case the floods were going to occur in the area on a regular basis. The Ministry of Steel and Mines sent a teleprinter message to the Northern Region of Geological Survey of India, Lucknow to geologically investigate the problem urgently and suggest remedial measures. I, from Photogeology and Remote Sensing Division and Mr Gautam Ghosh, from Quaternary Geology Division were entrusted with the job with instructions to submit our report expeditiously.

We interpreted the aerial photographs covering parts of Sahibi River Basin and adjoining areas in Gurgaon district of Haryana. We also studied satellite imagery for gaining a regional perspective. It was tentatively concluded that the area has near zero slope and had only Najafgarh drain, which was inadequate to drain the area efficiently. Sahibi River is a misfit stream losing flow in the desert margin of Rajasthan. However, a field check was necessary to arrive at a firm conclusion and suggest remedial measures. We had to wait for clearing of water from the waterlogged areas. Therefore, we could go for field work only in the first week of January '77. Our first camp was at the Bird Sanctuary at Sultanpur in Gurgaon district.

It was very cold when we started our work in the morning. The temperature dropped to sub-zero level and we could hardly hold our pencil to note down our observations. However, after being in the sun for a while, we resumed our work. By about 10 AM, we reached a large pond, where fish was being collected. I approached the owner with a 'Jai

Hind Chaudhary ji' salutation and asked whether he could sell a fish for us. He refused point blank. We were a bit taken aback. Suddenly, he enquired who we were and what we were doing. I narrated to him about the recent floods in the area and the follow up surveys we were doing for suggesting remedial measures. He yelled for one of his workers and commanded that one big fish be dropped in 'Hab's (Sahib's) jeep. He told me that it is a gift from him for us as we were guests, surveying the area for a good cause. We thanked him and proceeded for further work along the road to Pataudi.

On our way, we gave the fish to a *dhaba* at Farrukhnagar for cooking the fish for lunch when we returned back from our traverse. We finished our work going beyond Pataudi and returned back to Farrukhnagar late in the afternoon. We had our lunch with deliciously prepared fish. We could consume only half of the fish and gave away the rest to the *dabawala*. We paid him for lunch, but he politely refused to take the money as we were leaving half of the fish for him. On our way back, we were wondering about the tough behaviour of Haryana people with such courtesy and fairness.

We stayed at the guest house for the next couple of days, finishing our work around the place. While we were leaving for the next camp, I saw the visitors' book, to note that Sardar Swarn Singh, former Foreign Minister Government of India and Dr Salim Ali, a reputed bird watcher and Ornithologist had stayed before us in this guest house. A set of old song records of K. L. Sehgal, the famous singer of yesteryears, was available at the guest house. Mr Gautam Ghosh, who was an intense fan of Sehgal's songs, used to enjoy these in the evenings. His Director was Mr M. N. Sehgal at that time. There was quite a confusion when he was talking about Sehgal Sahib. I used to ask Gautam Ghosh as to which Sehgal he was referring to.

❑

37

Snowfall at Manali

Mr B. P. Mukherjee and I were assigned 'Snow Cover Study in Beas Valley' in the Field-Season 1976-77. This involved collection of old meteorological data from India Meteorology Department (IMD) at New Delhi and subsequently from Meteorology Station at Manali. We went to Deldhi by the end of March and stayed there for about a week and collected the relevant data from IMD. After the job was done we proceeded to Chandigarh by train. Arrangements were made that a vehicle will be provided from the GSI office at Chandigarh for carrying out our work at Manali. The train reached Chandigarh in the morning as per schedule and we were received by the driver, an ex-serviceman. After getting fresh and having a heavy breakfast, we started our onward journey.

We had lunch at a roadside dhaba near Mandi and reached Pandoh Dam on Beas River in the afternoon. The study aimed at finding the snowmelt contribution in Pandoh reservoir from the upstream snow cover. It took some time to meet officials at Pandoh damsite, consequently we left for an onward journey to Kullu in the late afternoon. Before Kullu, we noticed heavy clouds on the mountain side and as we moved further it started raining. On approaching Kullu, which is located at around 1200 m above mean sea level, the rain turned into a hail storm. We stopped for a while at a convenient and safe place, waiting for the severity of the storm to be reduced. As it was getting dark, I asked the driver, a sikh gentleman, whether we could proceed further. Looking at the low intensity of the hail, he responded enthusiastically also as our destination was not far from Kullu. We started further up the road for Manali. After a while it started snowing. The surroundings became very quiet and pleasant (due to release of latent heat while snowing). On approaching Manali the snowfall became severe but we kept moving on as the lights of Manali town were now visible. We reached Manali around 9:00 pm. The first thing which came to our mind was food as the streets were already deserted and most of the restaurants were closed. Suddenly we noticed that a restaurant was in the process of closing down. We stopped and approached the manager for food, who allowed us in. He told us that only chicken and rice was available for dinner but no tandoori roti as the tandoor was closed by then. We were happy with the proposition and ordered food for all three of us. Mukherjee enjoyed it the most.

After the meals, we proceeded towards the Municipal Guest House as per the direction given by the manager, where we were supposed to stay. On reaching there we found the guest house locked and the chowkidar had left the place due to severe inclement weather. It was still snowing. The next option was to go to the Public Works Department (PWD) guest house. We enquired from scant people around on the roadside. They directed us to move on the opposite side for about a kilometre. We reached there sooner only to find that it was also closed. However, the gate was not locked. We opened the gate and parked our vehicle in the portico and sighed with relief that our vehicle is now parked safely within Government premises. We looked for the chowkidar and shouted for him but to no avail. We thought of spending the night in the vehicle or in the open verandah. I moved in the verandah looking for a suitable corner where the effect of wind is least. Suddenly I noticed that the room no. one, though locked but the lock was below the roller. I removed the roller and opened the room. In the torchlight I saw that a double bed was nicely made with clean white sheets and blankets. A matchbox and a candle was also properly put on the window sill. I called for Mukherjee and the driver in sheer excitement and lit the candle. They could not believe their eyes and asked me time and again as to how I opened the room. Soon we got our sleeping bags and made ourselves comfortable. The driver managed himself in the changing room opposite the bathroom.

Next morning when we got up and strolled around, we found the snow had stopped possibly a couple of hours back. Our vehicle was under last night's snow. The driver tried to remove part of the snow from the vehicle's rooftop. Suddenly the chowkidar appeared and started shouting as to how we had opened the gate and occupied one of the rooms, without any permit. I pacified him by telling that we are officers of the Government of India. We can always park Government vehicle within the State Government premises for its safety. I asked him whether he was under the influence of liquor the previous evening while locking the doors, as one lock was below the roller. On seeing the condition of the lock, he realised his mistake and was profusely apologetic. I told him that we had reservations at the Municipal Guest House but it was locked due to severe weather conditions. We can meet the Executive Engineer for regularising our night's stay. He agreed that if we move to the Municipal Guest House soon there would be no need for meeting the Executive Engineer. He was apprehensive that we might report his negligence in performing his duty. Within an hour we moved to the Municipal Guest House. I tipped the chowkidar while leaving the PWD guest house, profusely thanking him for his 'mistake'. In my heart, I thanked Providence for saving us from the ordeal of cold through the mistake of the chowkidar.

❑

38

Jeep Accident

Mr R. V. Iyer and I were on another field assignment the following year in the Tehri area of Uttar Pradesh, now in Uttarakhand. After successfully completing the job, we closed our camp and started our journey to headquarters Lucknow, early in the morning with our camp equipment and baggage loaded in the trailer of the jeep. Our contingent money has nearly exhausted. We didn't renew the same as we were confident of reaching Lucknow, if everything went well. Our driver Mr R.A. Tewari, an ex-serviceman, could be considered an efficient driver, for his age of around 55 years.

After an arduous journey in the foothills of the Himalaya, we emerged in the Ganga plain at Bijnor. The onward journey was smooth as the road was good and the climate was pleasant in early October. We soon crossed Rampur and Bareilly and were heading towards Shahjahanpur by noon. At one spot the road took a slight curvature, where we saw a group of buffaloes grazing on one side of the road, while their keeper boys were lying on the road on the other side, under the shade of a tree in a relaxed mood. The vehicle was running rather fast.

Suddenly, one buffalo started trying to cross the road to join the group grazing across the road. Our driver swung the vehicle to the right, lowering its speed, to avoid the collision with the buffalo. He had to make a left swing again in order to save the boys lying on the road. Since the trailer load was heavy, the vehicle turned turtle. In the process, the hook of the trailer got broken and it fell on one side of the road. As soon as the trailer got detached the vehicle turned upside down again due to loss of momentum and we found ourselves in an upright position in the middle of the road. All this happened in about ten seconds. The vehicle has stopped. We were shocked and stunned. After a while, we asked the driver if he was alright. We all three were checking our limbs for any injury. Soon we came out of the vehicle intact without any major injury.

The boys on the road got up and rushed towards us after witnessing the plight of our vehicle. The vehicle was on its four wheels, however, the detached trailer had fallen on one side. We lifted it with the help of the boys. The wooden boxes containing office stationery and kitchen material were partly damaged. We put the tarpaulin covering the trailer in its place. Since the hook of the trailer got detached, it had to be fastened with rope to the back of the vehicle. After completing all this arrangement, we started the vehicle and moved slowly towards Shahjahanpur which was about five kilometres away. In about half an hour's time, we reached the city with few hiccups in our movement. Luckily for us, a mechanical shop was there on the outskirts of the city by the roadside. We got the hook welded, paying just fifty rupees.

Now we were left with a very meagre amount of money to manage the rest of the journey of about 150 km to Lucknow. We had no choice but to have tea with light snacks only for a delayed lunch. We reached our residences at Lucknow late in the evening, still thanking God for saving us from a major mishap.

❑

39

Ceremonial Parade at Srinagar

In the summer of 1978, I was deputed to the GSI Training Institute Camp at Srinagar, J. & K., as Instructor for the batch of officers of GSI, who could not be trained earlier. The camp was located near Rawalpora on the way to Srinagar Airport. This batch was a mix of young and old officers, hence families were officially allowed to stay in the camp, which had a decent tent colony. My family also joined me when schools were closed for summer holidays. My two daughters and son, aged 10, 9 and 7 years, respectively, enjoyed this trip by visiting many places in Kashmir valley. They enjoyed summer fruits, like plums, cherries, apricots, raw walnuts, raw almonds and green apples, available in plenty. The sojourn came to an end by the last week of June, as I had booked their return tickets to Lucknow, from the Out Agency, located at the Tourist Reception Centre (TRC), Srinagar, well before their scheduled opening of schools in the first week of July.

The bus journey from TRC, Srinagar to Jammu Railway Station takes almost 14 hours. The buses leave around 6:00 AM to catch the night train at Jammu. Therefore, we left our camp early in the morning at 5:30 AM. The then Prime Minister of India Sri Morarji Desai had come to Kashmir Valley and he was to be given an official send-off that day. There was a big police contingent, lined up on Hari Singh High Street, waiting for the arrival of the Prime Minister. Our driver, a Sardar ji, was a bit sleepy and before he realised the pose of police force, he rammed our jeep in the back of a police officer standing there instructing the police contingent. The vehicle just touched him, but that was enough to incense the whole police force who rushed towards our vehicle to manhandle the driver. No sooner this happened than the siren started blowing indicating the arrival of the Prime Minister. The police immediately rushed back to regroup in a line in attention. They, however, shouted back at our driver with choicest abuses to get back with our vehicle and move fast by the side lane. We complied and rushed to TRC taking side lanes just in time to catch our bus to Jammu Railway Station.

Soon all my family members boarded the bus and I checked their luggage and tickets for the onward journey, I sighed with relief and prayed to God very earnestly for this miraculous escape from a very unpleasant mishap. The driver surely would have been beaten up thoroughly and locked up in the police custody for his reckless driving. Our journey to Jammu and onward journey to Lucknow would have gone haywire. Thank God that we escaped this nightmare.

❑

40

Snakebite in Nagarjuna Sagar Area

I was deputed as Instructor for the Advanced Course in Photogeology and Remote Sensing run by GSI Training Institute at Hyderabad, in the summer of 1979. Photo-interpretation of aerial photographs covering areas close to Nagarjuna Sagar Dam, built across Krishna River, in Nalgonda district of the then Andhra Pradesh, was carried out. This was to be followed by a three days' field checks to be completed by the Officer Trainees by visiting the area. I and Mr. Mohammad Ahmad, who was Officer-in-Charge of the Course, accompanied the Officer Trainees and travelled to Nagarjuna Sagar on a day in the last week of August. We stayed at the Project Guest House at Nagarjuna Sagar.

Next day we went for field checks in the nearby area occupied by sedimentary rocks of Cuddapah Basin. The limestone rocks of this sequence are utilised in the cement factory of Macherla located not far away. By about noon, I realised that one of my socks on my right leg got excessively wet. I took off my hunter shoe to notice that some colourless fluid is oozing out from my ankle. There was no pain. The oozing did not stop even though I wiped it out a couple of times. Mr Mohammad Ahmad, who had worked in this area extensively, informed us that there were plenty of snakes in these areas roaming about especially during the summer and opined that my oozing could be due to a snake bite. He decided that the field work would be stopped forthwith and I should be rushed to the Primary Health Centre at Macherla.

The doctor at PHC, Macherla examined me thoroughly. I had not fainted till then and also I did not feel any symptoms of drowsing. He declared that it was not a case of snakebite. It was possible that some insect has bitten me on the ankle which had swollen by then and the bite could not go below the skin due to hunter shoes. We all sighed with relief and after minor first aid and waiting for some time, I was discharged from the clinic. Soon we reached our guesthouse at Nagarjuna Sagar and rested for the day. I was fine the next day and could resume our work for the next couple of days happily.

❑

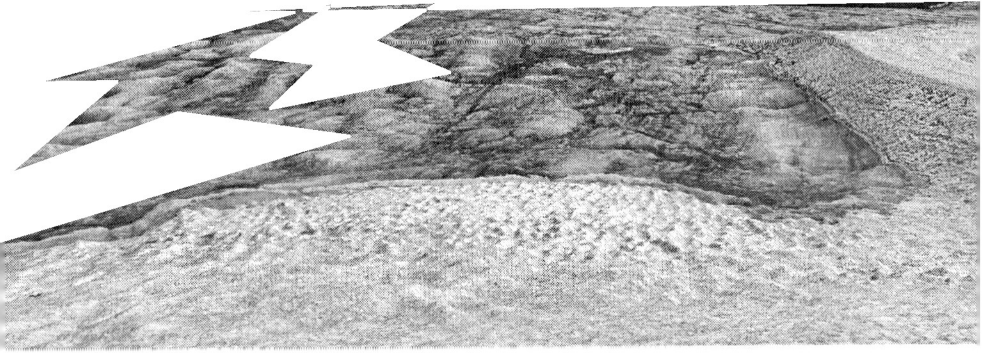

41

Crossing of an Icefan Near Chandanwari

After a heavy downpour and consequent flooding in 1978, the Rawalpora camp of GSI Training Institute was relocated at Aishmuqam in Liddar Valley of Kashmir in 1979. It was also necessary in view of a proposed highway, which was passing through the middle of the camp area. Mr B. D. Dungrakoti was the officer-in-charge of the Camp. The camp was located close to the stratigraphic sequences of Palaeozoic and Mesozoic Era, exposed in Liddar Valley. I was among the stalwarts like O. N. Bhargava, S. V.

Srikanthia, Gopendra Kumar, Gopal Singh and others, who had done extensive work in different parts of the Himalayas. We assembled at Aishmuqam Camp in early July' 80. Joint traverses were undertaken to establish stratigraphy and locate points of observation for Officer Trainees on these traverses. At the end of the week, after much deliberations, a uniform stratigraphy of the area was evolved and work started in the next week, when officers of the fourth orientation course arrived in the camp. I had known this batch rather well as I was associated with them at Raipur Camp.

We completed our task of imparting training in geological mapping and establishing order of superposition of the rocks, exposed in the area by middle August, by taking a batch of four to five officer trainees for each traverse and rotating them in different groups of Instructors. At the end, all the officer trainees were to be taken to Nehnar glacier for glaciological studies. A GSI camp was already established by the Glaciology Division of Northern Region, near Panjtarni close to the snout of the glacier. We all went there by trekking from Chandanwari onwards for a distance of about 20 kilometres. After three days of work most of us went to the holy Amanath cave and had darshan there. Mr D. B. Ghosh, Director J. & K. Circle accompanied us with his family.

We completed the return journey in one day, as it was going down the slope. However, we could reach Chandanwari by evening only. We had to negotiate a large ice fan at Chandanwari before reaching the roadhead, where our vehicles were parked to take us to our basecamp at Aishmuqam. Some of the officer trainees negotiated it, however, many of them, including wives of officer trainees and lady officers, found it difficult due to approaching evening as the fan surface became slippery. Mr Dhall and I went as an advance party making footsteps with the help of ice axes in a zigzag pattern. We rescued the trainees one by one holding their hands till they reached the foot of the fan, where they could manage on their own. The whole process took almost two hours. It was a great satisfaction that the rescue operation finished without any mishap. On reaching camp we were profusely thanked by the officer trainees and their families for rescuing them.

This batch left for Chitrdurga soon after. The next batch joined us after a few days. In the intervening period Gopal Singh and I had gone on a traverse to examine some rocks suspected of containing fossils. To our great excitement we discovered plant fossils, occurring at the margin of erstwhile Gondwana Continent. We took it as a reward for our visit to the holy cave and rescuing our fellow officers. The discovery was published as a research paper in the forthcoming seminar at Hyderabad.

❑

42

Aerial Photography of Gola Catchment Area

I had joined Remote Sensing Application Centre (RSAC), U.P. at Lucknow in March 1983. Aerial photography was planned for the Gola River catchment area and adjoining *Terai* belt of eastern Uttar Pradesh, in April that year. Soon a survey aircraft from National Remote Sensing Agency (NRSA, now National Remote Sensing Centre) landed at Amausi Airport. The weather at Amausi and the area to be photographed was all clear. The time of photography was decided to be between 9:30 and 10:30 A. M. to coincide with the Sun Synchronous LANDSAT satellite of NASA, USA. The season of photography before the beginning of summer was chosen to have least vegetation cover, as such good for geological purposes.

I and Mr Kachhwaha of Forestry Division were asked to accompany Prof Chaturvedi, The Director, RSAC. We reached Amausi Airport around 8:30 in the morning. After some formalities we all boarded the plane. It was Cessna Air survey Aircraft; small, light but roomy enough to accommodate 3 to 4 persons besides the pilot and the navigator. The navigator checked the camera, the film and all other parameters. Everything was found in perfect condition. The navigator cum-co-pilot went inside the cabin, while we kept our maps open to correlate with the ground as seen from the glass window near the camera, which was mounted to look down vertically. The plane took off soon and we acquired proper height in order to maintain the scale of the photographs. The day was perfectly clear and after being in the air for a while, we reached the area to be photographed. The navigator sighted the landmark for the first flight line and started taking photographs at regular interval to have desired forward overlap.

After the first flight line was completed the plane went ahead and took a turn around. The return flight was a dry run during which on board management of film and fixing other camera parameters was done to suit the requirements. After second turn around, we poised for the second flight line. The navigator sighted the landmark for the second flight line and steadied the plane towards it. The photography was carried out at intervals fixed like in the first flight line, maintaining proper side overlap. We were thrilled to see the geological and geomorphological features on the ground. A wide fan was visible along Gola River, where it debouches in the plain from the Himalayan foot hills. A fault was clearly seen cutting across the fan. The whole area was covered by photography by taking three or four more sorties. After having done our job, we headed towards Amausi Airport again for a safe landing there.

We touched down the runway by about 11:30 in the noon. In those days, the airport was operating only few flights, between Lucknow and Delhi, there was hardly anybody except the ground staff. We had our lunch in the lounge and thanked the pilot and navigator of the survey aircraft for successfully completing the task. They assured us that the photo prints will be made available to us in about a fortnight from the NRSA Laboratory. Prof. Chaturvedi was quite satisfied with the job done. After dropping him at his residence, we reached our residences filled with thrill and joy for actually taking part in an aerial photography, which we read in our text books so far.

❑

43

Enquiry in a Geophysical Work Contract

The Remote Sensing Application Centre (RSAC) entered into a contract with a Lucknow based firm for carrying out Geophysical Survey in Bundelkhand area in Jhansi District, for locating groundwater in perennially drought stricken area of the region. The ground surveys coupled with the aforementioned geophysical surveys lead to locating copious groundwater in limited aquifers of the area. It was a matter of jubilation for our groundwater team based at Jhansi and it attracted attention of the press also. The success was much appreciated at the headquarters Lucknow as well as by the State Government.

A kind of laxity prevailed and subsequent geophysical work was not carried out well by the contracting firm. The results were not satisfactory and the firm was asked to repeat the survey lines with due accuracy. The firm, however, stated that the work has been done satisfactorily and demanded their full and final payment. After some correspondence on the matter between RSAC and the contracting firm, the latter threatened to go for litigation if full and final payment was not made within certain stipulated period. A departmental enquiry committee was constituted to investigate the matter. The committee included a professor of Geohydrology, of Roorkee University (now IIT, Roorkee), a professor of Geophysics from Benaras Hindu University and myself from the RSAC. I was the Member Secretary of the Committee. We had a couple of meetings at Roorkee and Varanasi and recommended part payment to be made to the firm for the work they had done satisfactorily. We also recommended that some works may be repeated as indicated by the RSAC. The firm accepted the part payment but insisted for full and final payment within the stipulated period. The firm finally filed a civil suit for getting their due.

I was asked to liaise with the Government Pleader, who incidentally was living in the same locality of Indira Nagar, where I lived at that time. A counter affidavit was to be prepared in association with our Administrative Officer Mr Rakesh Chandra. One evening, Rakesh Chandra came to Indira Nagar to show a draft of the counter affidavit to the Government Pleader. Since he was returning back home from the office, he purchased some leafy vegetables *en route* and kept it in the front basket of the scooter where the file was already kept. He parked the scooter near the gate of the Pleader's house and pressed the bell. After waiting for a while, when there was no response, he opened the gate and went inside the house, presuming that he may be sleeping inside. The door was locked, therefore he returned back to the gate. To his utter dismay, he found two stray cows were eating the leafy vegetable from the scooter basket, while the other one eating the file. He shouted around and with difficulty could get half eaten file from the running away cow.

He came to my house to report the whole matter to me. I had gone out for some errand and my son, a teenager at that time, opened the door and asked him to sit in the drawing room and wait. Mr Chandra appeared a bit perplexed, so my son offered a glass of water and asked about his problem. After listening to his story, he could not stop his laughter and ran away to his room to have a laugh to his heart content. In the meanwhile, I had returned and we discussed the situation over a cup of tea. I suggested that the torn pages may be restored from the master file and other sources. The matter need not be brought to the notice of the Director and I will seek an appointment with the Pleader for next day morning before going to the office for examining the counter affidavit. He went back to the office and toiled for the next couple of hours to restore the file.

❑

44

Altercation between Two Scientists

The Remote Sensing Application Centre (RSAC) had established an office at Jhansi for carrying out groundwater investigation in Bundelkhand area in the year 1983. A Geophysics Division was added subsequently to support ground surveys. As the work progressed, more scientists were appointed and attached to the Division. Work was going on smoothly, till one day we received news at the headquarters Lucknow that there was an altercation and fighting between two scientists of Geophysical Division at Jhansi. This was a serious matter of indiscipline and I was asked by the Director, RSAC to rush to Jhansi and enquire about the matter and submit report to him for further necessary action.

I left for Jhansi the very next day and reached the office in the late afternoon and learned about the incidence from different local sources. I issued notices to the two scientific officers and others, who were witness to the incidence, to be present before me the next day and record their statements about the said incidence. On the next day, I cross questioned the officers involved and recorded their statements. The statements of the witnesses were also recorded. The aggrieved officer also showed me his T-shirt with a mark of hunter shoe on it. A typist-cum-clerk from administrative section was deputed to assist me in this task. I returned back to Lucknow by the night train, carrying all the relevant papers from Jhansi Office.

By the time I reached Lucknow, I was quite clear in my mind about the matter. The erring officer, being of short temperament, over reacted to a trivial provocation by the aggrieved officer. In my enquiry report, which was submitted a couple of days later, I came to the aforementioned conclusion. The erring officer was reprimanded with a warning not to repeat such misbehaviour in future and be more cordial towards colleagues. He was subsequently transferred to headquarters at Lucknow.

I visited Jhansi after sometime for examining some geological problem. I accompanied the same aggrieved officer to examine weathered outcrops of basic volcanic rock in an area south of Mau Ranipur. We gathered good number of evidences and collected samples to prove that the Deccan volcanic rocks extended far up in the north, generating a typical soil (chromustert) after weathering. On examining the relevant satellite imagery, we could establish the soil type at specific elevation to be the remnant of Deccan volcanic rocks. We submitted a scientific paper on the subject and presented it in the Indian Society of Remote Sensing Seminar at Vishakhapattanam. This discovery was much acclaimed then.

I encouraged and advised the young officer that the moral be learnt from the unpleasant incident was to forget and forgive and move on. As an intelligent person, he took the positive advice in right spirit. He subsequently went back to his parent organisation (ISRO) and flourished into a scientist of repute.

❑

45

Dadua Gang Episode

After the successful launch of Aryabhatta (1975), Bhaskara-I(1979) and Bhaskara-II(1981) satellites, the Indian Space Research Organisation (ISRO) was preparing to launch Indian Remote Sensing Satellite (IRS). Various user organisations, including Geological Survey of India (GSI), were involved in collecting spectro-radiometric data of their areas of interest so that sensors sensitive to the useful band of the spectrum could be developed for the proposed IRS. The GSI was to collect spectro-radiometric data for different rock types, for which an item in the Field Season Programme for the year 1986-87 was included for every Region of GSI. A workshop cum training programme was organised in August-September '86 at Bangalore. The instruments related to this survey were also distributed to each Region at the conclusion of the Training. Mr K. Krishnan Unni, Director, GSI, was the nodal officer of this activity.

Mr R. V. Iyer and I were given this responsibility in the Northern Region. We selected Lalitpur district, Uttar Pradesh, as it had different types of rocks exposed in the area, like Bundelkhand Granite (plutonic), Vindhyan Sandstone, Limestone and Shale (sedimentary) and Deccan Trap (volcanic). After studying about the rocks of this area and making necessary preparations, we left for Lalitpur district of Uttar Pradesh (U. P.), in Feb '87. Our first camp was at the PWD guest house at Gona close to the Madhya Pradesh (M. P.) border. We reached there rather late in the evening, and therefore, no food was available at the guest house. We asked the watchman of the guest house what to do about our dinner. He suggested that there was a *dhaba* a couple of kilometres away at the border of U. P. and M. P., where food was available. We all went there hurriedly lest the *dhaba* is also closed.

Soon we reached the *dhaba*. It was well lit with petromaxes and was rather clean. I asked the person there if we could get some food. He told me that we can get anything we want. I asked whether we could get chicken curry. He said anything and everything is available. We ordered chicken curry wondering at the same time how come at this hour of the night and at such a solitary place all types of food is available. However, we enjoyed the delicious food served to us. The prices were reasonable. I enquired whether we can have food the next day also. His reply was affirmative.

46

Night Halt in a Village House

A programme of investigating mineral resources with the help of remote sensing techniques was launched by the Geological Survey of India during the Field-Season 1990-91. Mr Arvind Misra and Mr S. C. Sharma were deputed with me to carry out this work in the Northern Region of GSI. We started our work of field checking in the southern part of Uttar Pradesh and in course of time we reached Mahoba, where we camped in the PWD guest house by the end of Jan' 91. We took a couple of traverses around Mahoba with our jeep.

Next day we took a traverse to Rath Tehsil of Mahoba district, along Kulpahar-Charkhari-Diha road. It was

I further asked casually as to how he is managing the dhaba profitably with lavish dishes and hardly any customers around. He told me that this area is frequented by the Dadua Gang of dacoits and there were express instructions to keep food prepared all the time. He further told me that they occasionally throw a bundle of currency notes in the *dhaba* enough to manage it profitably. We were a bit panic stricken, especially Mr. Iyer and the driver. I reassured them while moving in the vehicle that if we mind our business, the dacoits generally do not harm and they must have got the news of our arrival in the guest house through the watchman. We reached our camp and slept.

Next couple of days we carried out our survey work peacefully with the help of two guide mazdoors and enjoyed the food at the *dhaba*. On the third day, I told the guide mazdoors that today we will be going along a tributary of the Jamni River. The guide mazdoors suggested we take some other traverse instead. I could guess that the gang was visiting that area and it was not safe for us to go that side. I immediately agreed to their suggestion and decided to cover the eastern part of the area. We finished our work in the next couple of days and moved to another camp safely.

❑

an unmetalled road beyond Charkhari. However, we could finish most of our work planned for the day by the afternoon. The remaining work was to be done near Diha. We suddenly noticed that one of the tyres of our vehicle got punctured. We pushed the vehicle to one side of the road. The driver took out the stepney from the back of the vehicle, but found that it had much less air pressure than required. Under the circumstances, we were totally stranded, waiting for any vehicle to help us. The road was not frequented by vehicles or cyclists and their chances of coming on the road appeared dimmer due to approaching evening and also because the area was infested by dacoits. There was not any habitation as far as we could see. After waiting for about an hour or so, we saw a bus coming from the Mahoba side. We stopped the bus and narrated our precarious condition and requested them to tow our vehicle up to the nearest village. We also told them that we were Government Officers and were camping at the Mahoba guest house. The bus driver agreed to our pleadings and towed our vehicle up to the village Diha. Incidentally this was their last stop also and after the night halt there, they were supposed to resume their duty back to Mahoba.

The crew of the bus prepared their meals in the open by burning wood and offered us *roti* and *sabzi*. We ate our supper with due gratitude. It was quite cold outside, our driver somehow managed to sleep within the jeep with meagre clothings. A village person of Rathor clan offered to take us to their house for a night's rest, which we thankfully accepted. We had a good amount of cash with us, which we were carrying in our portfolio bag. We pretended that the bag had official papers and it was necessary to carry the bag, moreover it could be used as a pillow. We somehow slept in the house with blankets provided by the owner, having apprehensions about the money all the time lurking in the back of our minds. We got up late in the morning, but happy to note that nothing untoward happened. Soon we went out to freshen ourselves and had brushed our teeth with traditional neem *datun*. A group of young children from the village swarmed around us, asking all sorts of questions about maps, mountains, rivers, floods and droughts. We satisfied their curiosity as far as possible. We desperately realised how there was a dearth of good teachers in the village schools.

The bus fellows prepared paranthas for morning breakfast, which they shared with us. They left for Mahoba by about 9 AM. We thanked them profusely for their help and hospitality, offering them some money, which they reluctantly accepted. I dispatched our driver with the first available transport to Rath with the punctured tyres and to get them repaired. He returned back by about noon by a private truck and fixed these in the vehicle. We reached Mahoba Guest house by 2 PM, to see that the watchman was about to go to the police station to lodge a missing report about us. He was relieved so much to see us back and intact. He was almost sure that we had been kidnapped along with the vehicle by the dacoits. After taking a good rest in the camp, we finished our work in the next couple of days and moved to the next camp. I was speculating all along that the famous Rathor clan of Kshatriyas of Bundelkhand might have originated from Rath.

❑

47

Meeting an Old Classmate at Madawara

After completing field work in Chhatarpur, Jhansi, Shivpuri, Chanderi and Lalitpur, we went to Madawara, a Tehsil level town of Lalitpur district, in the last week of February '91. We had booked a PWD guest house at Madawara for our stay there, but on reaching there we were told that only one room is available to us as the other suite is booked for one Superintendent of Police (SP) of State Crime Investigation Department. We kept our luggage in the room and went for our work towards Sonrai village. On our return journey we had our dinner early, since it was already evening, and reached the guest house for the night's stay. I called on the SP and to my utter surprise he was none other than Avadhesh Bahadur Singh, a pal and classmate of my Intermediate College at Rae Bareli (U.P.). We hugged each other calling by first names. We exchanged our old memories of how he won the best athlete award in the district sport meet and how I was a favourite student of our mathematics teacher and used to help him check maths answer books of our class. My friend A. B. Singh invited us for dinner, but we politely declined as we already had our dinner. He then asked us to join him for breakfast the next day, to which we gladly agreed.

It was a lavish breakfast, where all available local cuisines including *Puree, Jalebi*, *Samosa*, a variety of sweets and fruits were served. While sipping our tea, I asked him what brought him to a remote place like this. He confided that there were reports of illegal marketing of Uranium ore from this area. I told him that the Atomic Minerals Division was exploring Uranium and other minerals in this area but without much success. The GSI is drilling for copper and related minerals near Sonrai, but with meagre success so far. He appeared satisfied and bade a warm goodbye, leaving that evening for his next destination.

After another day's work we shifted to a forest guest house far away from Sonrai. It was somewhat dilapidated and perhaps nobody visited the place for quite some time, due perhaps to the dacoit menace prevailing in the area. We hurriedly finished our work here just in a day to move to Sonrai.

We covered the area around Sonrai in a couple of days. Sonrai is known for *chironj*i, which grows on trees smaller than mango tree with leaves like that of *Mahua* tree. It has flowers like mango tree, but the flowering season is in early January. The fruits have a nut which is baked and the seed inside is *chironj*i, which is smaller than pea. Since the Holi festival was close by, we purchased some *chironj*i for consumption at home.

❑

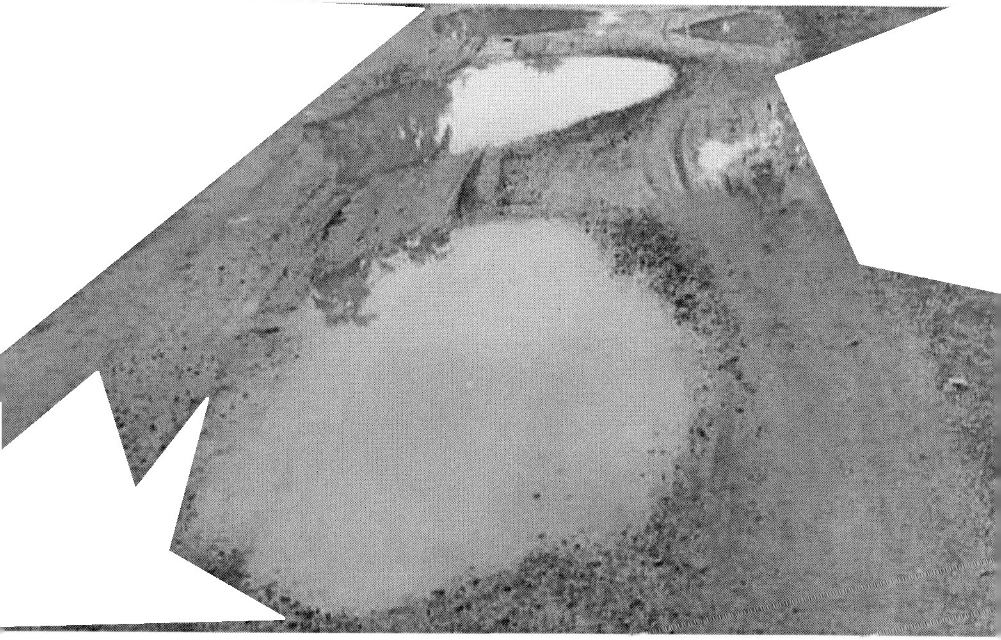

48

Negotiating a Damaged Road Near Bijawar

In the second year of Project Bhusampada, I had to carry out field checks of two and multiple lineament intersection points and associated mineralisation if any, in Panna, Chattarpur, Tikamgarh and Bijawar areas of Madhya Pradesh along with Sri Arvind Misra and Sri Satish Chandra Sharma. We started our work in January '92 and before reaching Bijawar, we finished work in the aforementioned three localities. We stayed in a forest guest house near Mungwari in late January and completed our work in the next couple of days taking traverses along unmetalled forest roads. Subsequently, we shifted our camp to Bijawar moving along a dilapidated forest road. After going for a distance of about ten kilometres, we found the road more damaged and it was difficult to negotiate that stretch of road. Sharma ji and our driver Kunne Khan were enthusiastic in proceeding further somehow. I thought that even if we negotiated that patch, one did not know about the road conditions further ahead. In that eventuality, one could not return back either. Therefore, we sent two of our guide mazdoors to find out the condition of the road up to Baksahwa, which was connected to Bijawar by a metalled road.

We waited there for about an hour till we got the news that the road ahead was passable by our jeep. Soon the driver boarded the jeep and Sharma ji started guiding him from the front to negotiate the patch. Rest of us followed the jeep. It was an arduous task but the skill and perseverance of Kunne Khan helped to manage it successfully. Very soon we boarded our jeep and reached Baksahwa, from where it was a smooth journey to Bijawar. The rocks around Bijawar were of much interest to us as they formed the 'type area' for 'Bijawar Group' in Indian Stratigraphy and were considered time equivalent of the Cuddapah Group of rocks occurring in Andhra Pradesh and Telangana.

We stayed at Bijawar for the next three days and examined a reported base metal mineralisation nearby. We also visited Bhimkund situated about 30 kilometres south of Bijawar. The Kund is located in a limestone cave of overlying Vindhyan rocks and as per local belief it is unfathomable and the Pandavas stayed there during their forest sojourn. We left Bijawar after finishing our work and proceeded to the Banda side in the east to continue our field checks in the Rewa- Hanumana-Sidhi area.

❑

49

An Incident with Mr Jero at Pushkar

During my posting as Director of Photogeology and Remote Sensing (PGRS) Division of GSI, Western Region at Jaipur, a collaborative programme with BRGM, France for Mineral Exploration was undertaken in 1992. The first phase of this programme was taken up in the Khetri Copper belt with Mr Kozminsky, an expert in Remote Sensing from BRGM. In the subsequent year, Mr Jero, a young person, joined for PGRS work in place of Mr Kozminsky. We had planned digital image processing work at Regional Remote Sensing Service Centre (RRSC),

Jodhpur in September '93. It was *'pitra paksha'*, a fortnight when Hindus pay homage to their dead ancestors at holy places. Pushkar is one such place where this type of pooja is performed during the aforementioned fortnight.

Mr Jero and I left Jaipur after breakfast and reached Ajmer by noon, on our way to Jodhpur. Since Pushkar is located close to Ajmer, we went there. Mr Jero went sightseeing along the Pushkar Lake, while I performed pooja, especially for my mother, whom we lost in 1987. After performing the pooja, I looked for Mr. Jero, who to my utter surprise was also performing pooja with the help of a Panda ji. Approaching them I asked Mr Jero in English whether his parents were alive. He nodded in afirmative. I explained to him that this pooja is performed by any person whose one or both the parents were dead. Then I turned to Panda ji and asked him in Hindi to stop the pooja as both of Jero's parents were alive. I asked Mr Jero to pay Rupees fifty one as 'Dakshina'in lieu of part of the pooja performed by him. Panda ji, though unwilling to accept dakshina, realised his mistake and took it after my persuasion. The matter settled amicably, and we proceeded for the onward journey to Jodhpur.

We reached Jodhpur by the evening and settled in a tourist guest house, booked for us by our office in advance. After doing our work in the RRSC Laboratory, we were returning to the guest house when Mr. Jero stopped the car near a *dhaba* where samosas were being prepared. He told me that he likes the samosa. I told him that Jodhpur samosas may have more chillies, but he not only enjoyed hot samosas but also tried chilli pakoras. I was a little worried that this may upset his stomach. However, I was reassured the next day, when he again stopped the car near the same *dhaba* to enjoy samosas and chilli pakoras. We returned back to Jaipur the next day after finishing our work. When I narrated about the Pushkar incident to our fellow scientists, they all enjoyed the *faux pas*.

❑

50

New Map Policy

I had to visit the Ministry of Steel and Mines quite often in the year 2002 in connection with digitisation of maps and preparation of database for Geological Survey of India (GSI) in collaboration with BRGM, France. I met Ms Adarsh Misra, IAS, the Additional Secretary, looking after the Department of Mines. GSI was an attached office to the Department of Mines. I was asked by her to give a presentation of the said project and problems faced during its implementation. I had hardly started my presentation, than she asked me to pause and called the Joint Secretary and a few Director level officers to participate in the presentation, as this was an important project which was going to change the handling of map and text data to a computerised platform. I gave details of bibliographic database and preparation of geoscientific database by digitisation of maps and reports as attached files.

I mentioned about the problems in the digitisation of base maps in restricted areas as it was prohibited by the Survey of India. The officers of the Ministry were satisfied with the talk and they left after a brief question-answer session.

The Additional Secretary wanted to know how to resolve this problem. I elaborated on the problem and told that although the concern of Survey of India is genuine on defence requirements, it is equally important to release the map data in digital format for public consumption. If they do not do that people have alternate access to such data from Google platform and the Survey of India (SOI) will lose revenue in the process. Being the Member of the Committee on formulating New Map Policy, she asked me to attend the next meeting with her to suggest a viable solution of the problem.

I went to Delhi again and met the Additional Secretary, Ministry of Mines and appraised her about my suggestion on the matter. I thought that the maps, prepared on Everest Ellipsoid, for defence purposes may remain restricted / secret, while the maps for public domain may be prepared on another Ellipsoid (WGS 84) and allowed unrestricted. The data from satellites and the Global Positioning System (GPS) are also displayed on WGS 84 Ellipsoid. Thus there will be good concurrence with this series of unrestricted maps. The data from Google platform is also on the same ellipsoid. She liked the idea very much and asked me to accompany her for the meeting. Soon we reached the Ministry of Defence, to which the Survey of India was an attached office and was a participant in the meeting.

During the meeting, I sat behind her, as per the decorum of the meeting. When her turn came to address, she asserted that the Survey of India had been sharing the restricted maps with the GSI so far and on that basis GSI were providing expert advice to Border Road Organisation (BRO). Now without having access to the digital data, how do they expect to their job, using modern techniques. The SOI expressed their anxiety of fast dissemination of digital data, hence difficult to enforce restriction in any effective manner. She then introduced me as the Deputy Director General, in-charge for preparing digital data base in the Northern Region of GSI and asked me to explain my point of view on the matter. I gave the idea what I had discussed with the AS, adding a proverb in Hindi that like an elephant there are 'Khane ke dant aur, dikhane ke dant aur'. Everybody in the meeting enjoyed the metaphor but also understood well the proposition of using two ellipsoids for different purposes.

After my superannuation in 2003, The New Map Policy was finalised and declared by the Government of India in 2005. It has the Defence Series of Maps (DSM) and an Open Series of Maps (OSM) prepared on the said ellipsoids, respectively.

❑

51

Convincing the Honourable Minister

Ms Uma Bharati was the Honourable Minister of the Ministry of Steel and Mines in the Government of India, in the year 2002, when I was Deputy Director General of Operation: Uttaranchal and Uttar Pradesh of Geological Survey of India, based at Lucknow. Tehri Dam was ready for operation, the upstream reservoir was getting filled and it needed a nod from our Honourable Minister. There was an uproar in the media at that time that the waters of Holy Bhagirathi River, on which the dam was constructed, was being contaminated due to the impounding of its water in the reservoir. The Honourable Minister wanted to see the area herself and made a programme of visiting Uttaranchal (now Uttara Khand) in

September that year to see the dam, besides her interest in having darshan of shrines of Uttaranchal. I was deputed by the Head of Department of Northern Region to arrange for the Minister's visit and make her aware of the activities of Geological Survey of India through lectures, exhibition and spot visits. I organised a team of Directors of my Operation heading Drilling, Glaciology, Mineral Exploration and Engineering Geology Divisions, for the job.

The Honourable Minister with her entourage arrived at Haridwar, as per schedule and we received her with enthusiasm and fan fair. Her personal Assistant, an IAS officer, was briefed about Duggalbitta camp near Tungnath at an altitude of about 3000 m (9000 feet) above mean sea level, as the Minister had desired that she wanted to see GSI camp life and would like to stay in a tent. We had accordingly got a tent pitched in the back of a guest house with mattresses and sleeping bags. If she felt uncomfortable in the severe cold of the night, she could as well move into the heated guest house through the back door. The entourage reached Duggalbitta at 5:00 pm. After a brief welcome ceremony over a cup of tea, we organised a lecture on Tehri Dam through a slide show, which was very successful, especially the question answer session which followed it. The interaction continued at the buffet dinner of *poori bhaji* around the campfire lit for the occasion. She liked the arrangements of night stay and preferred to stay in the tent. I and a few senior officers left for Ukhimath camp for our night's stay.

The next day a lecture was delivered by me at Kalimath Vidyapith campus on the origin of the Himalayas. The lecture was a bit too long, however, the Honourable Minister listened to it with rapt attention, sitting in '*Padmasana*' posture on the sofa. The later part of the lecture included the evolution of man, which I tried to shorten as it was getting late for the next programme on the schedule. Uma Bharti ji asked me to continue in detail, unless I am tired. I continued for another half an hour talking about different phases of the Ice Age and the advent of man (Homo sapien). After a couple of days, she decided to visit the Vishnuprayag Hydel project on the way to Badrinath. She first visited Musk Deer Park on the way between Chopta and Rudraprayag. At the park, the Honourable Minister posed a riddle, written by Saint Kabir of mediaeval era, as the musk deer searches for the musk smell in the jungle, while it is residing in his navel. She wanted us to complete the next line. At first, none of us could recollect the next line of the couplet. Suddenly I remembered it and said that God is within us while we try to look for Him outside. She was mighty pleased and wondered if I knew Hindi literature also besides Geology.

We moved on to Rudraprayag, where the Honourable Minister had a meeting with the local party workers. Leaving them there, we officers from GSI proceeded to the Vishnuprayag hydel project in advance and awaited her arrival. The entourage of the Honourable Minister arrived at the head of penstocks around 4:00 pm, where she was greeted by the staff of the construction company. I explained the scheme of the project and actually showed her how only part of the water from Alaknanda River is going into the penstocks to generate electricity using the force of gravity, in the power house located about 1000 feet below. The water joins Alaknanda River again, uncontaminated. I further explained to her that the Tehri Dam project is also having a similar scheme. Once the reservoir of Tehri dam is filled, the amount of water of Bhagirathi River which comes to the reservoir goes through relatively larger penstocks and generates electricity through gravity in the powerhouse below. Finally the same amount of water goes back to Bhagirathi River. The present lean flow of Bhagirathi River below the dam is only transient till the reservoir is full. She was impressed and seemed satisfied with both the projects and soon left for Badrinath.

After having Ḍarshan at Badrinath temple the next day, we left for our next destination, the Kaliasaur Landslide Zone, on the way to Haridwar. A brief talk on the landslide and its remedial measures was given by the Director Engineering Geology Division. Before her departure for Haridwar, the honourable Minister, thanked us for accompanying her on a long trip which she profusely enjoyed. As Dussehra festival was on the next day, she asked us not to come to Haridwar to see her off, instead proceed to our homes to join the festivities. She said to me as a parting remark, that she was convinced that there is no contamination of Bhagirathi River due to Tehri Dam and would allow its functioning as soon as the reservoir is full. This was a matter of great satisfaction to me.

❑

52

Visiting Professorship in Bundelkhand University

My son got married in the month of February 2003 and I retired from my service in the Geological Survey of India, at the end of the month in the same year. I was busy with the post marriage functions of my son during the following couple of months and rested subsequently. Prof. S. P. Singh, Head of Geology Department of Bundelkhand University contacted me for delivering lectures in Remote Sensing for their new batch of M. Sc. Students, as a Visiting Professor, commencing in August '03. I declined the offer in view of prevailing rule that I could not take any appointment within a year of my retirement. I had known Prof. Singh in connection with a project he submitted to the Ministry of Mines for a grant, which was approved by the then Honourable Minister Ms Uma Bharti. In the meanwhile, I was appointed by the

Ministry of Mines as chairman of the Monitoring Committee of the project for two years. After the tenure of the committee was over, I went to Jhansi in the month of September '05 and stayed in the International Guest House of Bundelkhan University for about ten days. I formulated the curriculum of the paper on Remote Sensing for M. Sc. and delivered lectures accordingly. Prof. Singh took me to the residence of the then Vice-Chancellor of Bundelkhand University, Prof. Ramesh Chandra and introduced me to him over a cup of tea. He told the Vice-Chancellor about my lectures and setting of the curriculum, etc. Prof. Chandra was impressed with my work and offered me the Visiting Professorship for a period of three years.

At the conclusion of the lectures, Prof. Singh wanted my opinion and advice on a groundwater recharge problem in the vicinity of Jhansi town. He took me on his scooter to the place near a pond, not far off from the town. The pond held water during the monsoon period and for a short period thereafter. It got dried completely during the summer months. His idea was to divert water from nearby streams to the pond for better groundwater recharge in turn to augment water supply to the town. We alighted from the scooter and started examining the soil and rocks near the pond. Suddenly a group of three or four students appeared on their motor bikes with hockeys in their hands. Without uttering a word, they started beating Prof. Singh. I shouted for help and tried to pacify the students. Prof. Singh fell on the ground with the sudden attack. Realising that he was grievously hurt, the students ran away on their bikes.

I was stunned and numb for a while. I went closer to Prof. Singh and lifted him up. He was by then a bit more composed and checked for his injuries. To our great relief, all his limbs were functioning alright, however, there were surficial injuries on his hands and back. I asked him whether he can sit on the pillion of the scooter. He nodded in affirmative and soon we boarded the scooter and I drove him to his residence. We gave him first aid and consulted a doctor nearby for medicines and proper bandages on the injury. On our return to his residence, Prof. Singh told me that he was also holding the charge of the Dean of Student Welfare. The miscreants were students of Bundelkhand University and perhaps some outsiders. There was some problem with their admissions. They felt aggrieved and took revenge on him. I asked him to take rest and be cautious for future. Wishing him quick recovery, I left the place as I had train reservation for my return journey to Lucknow same night.

On reaching my home at Lucknow, I narrated the whole incidence to my wife. She thanked God that I escaped unhurt in the unpleasant episode. I was a bit hesitant in accepting the teaching assignment there. She allayed my fears by saying that these were stray incidents and I should not give up the visiting professorship offer in Bundelkhand University. Subsequently, I accepted the offer and continued there for the next couple of years with very pleasant memories of academic activities.

❑

53

Digitization of Data in an Irrigation Department

During my visit to Jhansi for assignment as an External Examiner in 2005, I was introduced to the Commissioner, Jhansi Division by Prof. S. P. Singh. In our discussion, the Commissioner learnt that I was actively associated with Database Management activity in the Geological Survey of India. Being a graduate from Indian Institute of Technology, Kanpur, the Commissioner showed keen interest in establishing a database system for the revenue offices under his control. He asked me to prepare a project proposal in this regard and submit the same to him. I prepared a detailed project report in a couple of months and submitted the same to him by the end of September '05. After some deliberations on my proposal, a date in January '06 was fixed for my lecture on Database Management and presentation on the Project Implementation.

I reached Jhansi on the appointed date and was lodged in the Circuit House of Jhansi. I delivered my lecture and presentation in the forenoon, which was well received and acclaimed. The Commissioner had asked all the District Magistrates and related officials to be present for the talk. He suggested that I select either Public Works Department (PWD) or Irrigation Department for establishing a digital database on pilot project basis. I preferred Irrigation Department due to my familiarity with Geohydrology.

I was taken to the Irrigation Department in the afternoon, where I met the Executive Engineer, who was present during my talk in the forenoon. We selected a small catchment and tried to locate the canals within the catchment area. I picked up a canal and wanted to have such information like when it was constructed, how much area it irrigates, how often the silt in the canal has been removed and about its cost details, etc. The office of the Executive Engineer was unable to provide this type of data immediately. They informed me that such data may be lying in some old files, which were inaccessible at that moment. We prepared a flow sheet and tried to put attributes for each canal, based on the expected quarries. I also wanted the canal and its distributaries plotted on a map. Finally, I asked them to extract data from their files on given attributes, so that a Relational Data Base Management System (RDBMS) could be developed using Oracle, Arc/Info and other software. The Irrigation Department promised me to collect and keep the data for me for the pilot project in the next couple of months.

On my subsequent visit to Jhansi, I found that the Commissioner, Jhansi Division had been transferred to his next posting and the next incumbent did not show much interest on digitisation and was not keen on proceeding further with the digitization project. I was sorry for his lukewarm attitude and thus a good opportunity of using new technology of Database Management was lost.

❑

54

Anomalous Water Divide of Bata and Markanda Rivers

The Geological Survey of India had celebrated 125th year of its establishment by organising seminars and exhibitions at different places of the country in the year 1976. A seminar was organised by the Northern Region of GSI at Nahan, in Himachal Pradesh in this process. This was to be followed by the inauguration of Suketi National Fossil Park located close by. While I was travelling in a jeep from Paonta Sahib on way to Nahan, along Bata River, I noticed suddenly that we had crossed the water divide to more rugged terrain of Markanda River. I had a habit of observing the road side while travelling in a vehicle; the habit still persists. I asked the driver to take me back for about half a kilometre to see the water divide again. I observed that the Bata River coming from north abruptly took an eastward turn in to a wide valley, along which we came. The water divide was so subtle in nature that it supported paddy cultivation (which requires flat area). The Markanda River also initially flowing from north took a turn toward the west. However, the Markanda Valley was narrower and the terrain more rugged. It appeared as if the water divide was of geologically recent in origin and was the result of neo-tectonic uplift. I continued my journey to Nahan, attended the seminar and the inaugural function of Suketi National Fossil Park. The impression of Bata-Markanda water divide remained in the back of my mind ever since.

Years passed by and I did not have the opportunity to visit this area again. During my last years of GSI, I was asked by the Honourable Minister Ms Uma Bharti to give two presentations in connection with the River Linking Project and The Vedic Saraswati River. The first presentation was not difficult as some work in that direction had already been carried out for Ken – Betwa Link Project in the Budelkhand region of Uttar Pradesh. I gave the presentation in the Ministry of Mines in due course, which was well received. I needed some time for the presentation on Vedic Saraswati River, as a lot of literature was available on the subject and the topic was hotly debated in the scientific community and in the media since a couple of decades back. The literature encompassed the works of a German author Wilhelmy (1969), Yashpal *et al.* (1980), Sahai (1999), Kochhar (2000), Puri (2001), Lal (2002) and many others. Geological Society of India had published a memoir on the Vedic Saraswai River in 1999 and my teacher Prof. K. S. Valdiya brought out a book on the subject in 2002. David Frawley (alias Vamdeva Shastri) of American Institute of Vedic Studies in California, USA, often wrote knowledgeable articles in the print media on the subject. All this literature was collected and collated to form a reasonably good presentation on the subject. As ill luck would have it, the Honourable Minister had resigned by the end of January '03 and I retired from GSI by the end of February, 2003.

In the meanwhile, I was elected Chairman of Lucknow Chapter of the Indian Society of Remote Sensing for the term (2002-04). This and other errands kept me busy during my post retirement period. I visited Lucknow University for attending the S.N. Singh Memorial Lecture in September '03, where I had met Prof. Indra Bir Singh. I knew him since my University days as he was a year senior to me. Subsequently, I had worked with him on Quaternary Deposits of Gomati River around Lucknow in 1976. I discussed with him about my interest in Vedic Saraswati River and the material I had collected in this connection. He suggested that if I was keen on the subject, I should join him as a Ph.D. scholar so that there is a time bound goal for carrying out the studies. I asked him to give me some time to make up my mind.

Soon thereafter, I started going to the Geology Department of Lucknow University and started focusing on Bata–Markanda river basins for analyzing their drainage morphometry, jointly with Dr. A.K. Kulshrestha, who had thorough knowledge in Arc/GIS computer software for measuring different parameters. We selected this area due to the lurking suspicion in my mind of neo-tectonic activity along the Bata-Markanda water divide and its proximity to a number of streams named Saraswati Nadi/River, at times disconnected and flowing intermittently through Punjab-Haryana Plain adjoining the Himalayan Foothills. Prof. I.B. Singh was impressed with my regularity and sincerity towards the study. However, he suggested that I should concentrate on a smaller area in the Punjab-Haryana Plain to bring out geomorphological implications of the Vedic Saraswati River. The research topic was decided and I was enrolled as a Ph.D. student in January, 2005. I visited Bata-Markanda area after nearly thirty years and carried out field checks, courtesy Prof. M.P. Singh, the then Head of Geology Department of Lucknow University. I and Kulshrestha prepared a research paper on the subject, which was scrutinized by Prof. I.B. Sigh. The paper was presented in Kangra Earthquake Centenary Seminar in April '05 and was published in the Special Publication of the Geological Survey of India, subsequently.

I was awarded Ph.D. degree for my thesis prepared under the guidance of Prof. I.B. Singh in 2009. Incidentally I was his last Ph.D. student. My researches continued even in post-doctoral period, especially on Ganga-Indus Water Divide[2].

2 For Indian Subcontinent, the water divide is significant in that, if a drop of water falls on the eastern side of the divide it goes to Bay of Bengal, while that on the western side goes to Arabian Sea. Demarcation of water divides is important for river linking projects and water management of the basins.

Jakhu[3] Hill is the highest point in Simla and the north-south ridge commencing from there demarcates Ganga-Indus Water Divide as Pabbar and Giri rivers flowing in the eastern direction contribute to Yamuna River of Ganga Basin, while the streams flowing to the west of the ridge contribute to Satluj River of Indus Basin. Likewise the Bata-Markanda water divide coincided with the Ganga-Indus Water Divide; Bata River contributes to Yamuna River, while Markanda River contributes to Satluj Basin. It was amazing to note that the cities of Kurukshetra and Delhi are sprawling on either side of the Ganga-Indus Water Divide; the Supreme Court building is precisely located on this divide.

❑

3 The word Jakhu is derived from 'Yaksha'. It is possible that Yaksha tribes were residing here in pre-historic times.

55

The Enigma of Lost Saraswati River at Prayag Raj

According to the Nadi Suktam Shloka of Rigveda, the Saraswati River flowed between Yamuna and Satluj rivers, through the modern states of Haryana, Punjab, Rajasthan along and in proximity of present day Ghaggar River course. The present day satellite images of the area reveal that the river further flowed from Anupgarh in Rajasthan to Fort Abbas in Pakistan disappearing subsequently in the Thar Desert. The River reappears in the Sindh Province of Pakistan along Hakra –Nara course, more or less parallel to the course of Indus River. The Saraswati River debouched finally in the Arabian Sea (Saraswat Sea of epic Mahabharata) through the Rann of Kachchh. In Vedic times, the mighty Saraswati River was having a perennial source of water in Har-ki-Dun group of Glaciers (as proposed by Puri, 2001). Satluj River, a perennial river emanating from Mansarovar Lake of Trans-Himalayan Region, was contributing to Saraswati River in Vedic times. In response to northward movement of Indian Tectonic Plate over Delhi-Ambala sub-surface high, the area got uplifted and lateral movement along Ropar tear fault, the Satluj River started migrating westward through number of palaeo-channels observed on Ropar mega fan. Vedic Saraswati River started showing signs of disruption owing to reduced rainfall and the tectonic activity in the region between 5000 to 4000 years BP (Before Present). At present Satluj River near Ropar takes a knee bend towards the west and joins Indus River System.

Block movement along Yamuna tear around the same time disrupted the Himalayan segment of Saraswati River. In our recent research paper (Srivastava and Kulshresths, 2020) we have, on the basis of geological evidences, postulated that the erstwhile Saraswati River was flowing along Giri-Bata-Markanda river courses as a single stream and the same was disrupted due to tectonic uplift, creating a new water divide. Thus much of head waters of Saraswati River were lost to Yamuna River. Presently both Giri and Bata rivers are contributing to Yamuna River. In the process, the downstream of Saraswati River became lean and desiccated.

During my fieldwork in the area, I visited a small Saraswati temple located at the head of Markanda River on the western side of Bata-Markanda water divide, mentioned above. The temple is among the Plaksh trees (Plaksh Prasar Van described in the epic Mahabharata) and a number of water springs, perhaps connected to the tectonic lineaments. The temple priest gave us food as Prsadam of the Deity. As a parting gift, he gave me an old book which mentioned the Pilgrimage of Balram ji, the elder brother of Lord Krishna, as described in the epic Mahabharata. Balram ji did not participate in the holy war of Kurukshetra as both Duryodhan and Bhim were his disciples while teaching them the art of mace war. Instead, he preferred to go to pilgrimage of holy places, located mostly in the Saraswati Basin. Markandey Ashram on the bank of Saraswati River was on the last leg of his trip. This further strengthened my view that Bata-Markanda once formed part of erstwhile Saraswati River. After having a dip in the holy Saraswati River at the Ashram, Balram ji received the news about the mace war between both of his disciples at the fag-end of the holy war. He then went to take a dip in Yamuna River flowing nearby. Garibnath Hill, near Paonta Sahib, probably formed the water divide between the Saraswati and Yamuna rivers then. After the dip and without crossing Yamuna River, Balram ji rushed on his chariot to Kurukshetra, which was also located west of Yamuna River, to watch the mace war between the two warriors and to ensure that it is fought on strict dharmic rules.

After the tectonic event in post Mahabharat era (about 5000 year BP), the new water divide was created within the Saraswati River, the Bata River carrying all head waters of Saraswati River and reversed its direction to the east to join Yamuna River. The huge amount of Saraswati water augmented the flow and the eroding power of Yamuna River leading to deepening its thalweg (depth). The combined water of Saraswati and Yamuna rivers reached Prayag Raj, the holy confluence of three rivers (Triveni), Ganga, Yamuna and Saraswati. One can notice the deeper blue water of Yamuna River as compared to whitish water of shallow Ganga River at the confluence. Geographically speaking, it is Ganga River which debouches in Yamuna River. Mughal emperor Akbar's Fort at Prayag Raj, located on the eastern bank of Yamuna River, has a well, named after Saraswati River. The guide there explains that the water of the well is that of Lost Saraswati River. The belief of people about the confluence of Triveni (Ganga, Yamuna and Lost Saraswai rivers) at Prayag Raj is perhaps based on the above facts.

❑

56

Nepal Earthquake of April 2015

I was associated with the University Grants Commission (UGC) since quite some time due to my expertise in the field of Remote Sensing. I was called to review project proposals involving Geology and Remote Sensing components. The process continued more often after my retirement from the service of Geological Survey of India (GSI) in 2003. After acquiring Ph.D. degree in 2009, the UGC gave me responsibilities in their other committees. I was appointed a Member for evaluating a post graduate college in Bangaluru for granting autonomous status, in 2011 and the likes, subsequently. I was nominated Chairman of the committee for recommending grants for construction of women hostels in post graduate colleges of different universities.

The UGC committee under my chairmanship visited different post graduate colleges attached to one university each in Odisha, West Bengal and Bihar in the year 2012 The UGC again asked me to chair the committee for recommending grants for construction of women hostels in post graduate colleges of Bhupendra Narayan Mandal University, Madhepura, Bihar in 2015. I went to Katihar by a direct train from Lucknow, in the month of April '15. I was received by a professor of B.N. Mandal University at Katihar railway station and was taken to Madhepura by road. I was lodged comfortably in a hotel at Madhepura. In the evening, I met the committee members and the Vice-Chancellor over a welcome tea party at his residence, where modus operandi of the work was finalised. In all, there were about twenty post graduate colleges which were granted funds for Women's Hostel, therefore, four to five colleges were to be visited every day for grant of further instalments.

The Committee started its work the next day and we were welcomed by 'Dahi- Chura' a favourite local dish of Mithilanchal containing curd, sugar and flattened rice served in the morning hours of summer months. The work went on smoothly for a couple of days. On the third day (25 April '15) about noon time, while we were proceeding to another college, a bit far away from Madhepura, we felt that the car was moving on a bumpy road. The driver was shocked and surprised about the jumping of the car, even though the road appeared very smooth. He quickly pulled the vehicle on one side of the road, stopped in panic and came out of the car, shouting that it was an earthquake. By the time we all got out of the car, the tremors stopped. It must have lasted for about ten seconds. I pacified the driver and appreciated his presence of mind to stop the car in an open area far from big trees. Soon we boarded the car and in the next half an hour we reached the college. There was commotion in the college campus and in the city streets through which we came. The college authorities welcomed in the usual manner although the topic of discussion was still the earthquake.

Soon we got down to the business. In my address to the members of the committee and its counterpart from the college, I dwelt for a while on the causes of earthquake. Thanks to social media, the information reached us that it was a major earthquake of 7.8 Magnitude. The epicentre was located at about 76 km northwest of Kathmandu in Nepal at a depth of 15 km below the surface. The earthquake was caused by the rupture along the Main Central Thrust (MCT) in the Central Himalayas. I briefly mentioned about the movement of Indian tectonic plate below the Eurasian plate. The disruption released a huge amount of energy causing shocks of vibration travelling through Primary (P-waves) and secondary or Shear waves (S-waves) leading to movement along and in perpendicular to the wave direction, respectively. However, the damage is mostly done by surface waves, which caused vertical and lateral movement causing shear cracks and damage to the built-up structures. The effect of earthquake reduces as one moves away from the epicentre. I also assured the audience that the scale of damage is likely to be less in Madhepura area due to excessive thickness of Ganga Alluvium in the proximity of Himalayan Foothills, being located in the 'Foredeep' of the Ganga-Indus Basin. In case of aftershocks, which were likely then, one should move out of the building to open area and for those who cannot run out should stay at the corner wall junction or below some furniture, saving their head. I had hardly finished my address than there was a shock again. Everybody ran out helter skelter. I again assured them that the intensity in aftershocks will be less than the main shock. It lasted for about 5 seconds and we resumed out meeting soon thereafter.

The newspapers on the following day were full of this tragic incidence. The rescue team from National Disaster Rapid Force (NDRF) and medical teams from India rushed to Nepal and performed their task very professionally. Other countries including China and United Kingdom also provided help in rescue operations. Nearly 9000 people died and about 20,000 were injured, besides the large scale destruction of property and infra-structure. A number of aftershocks were recorded but the biggest was on 12th May'15, which had 7.3 Magnitude. It again caused damage to the lives and property. As a child, I was wondering all the while, as to why the wooden pillars of front veranda of our ancestral house were tilted and broken and needed support by brick pillars on either side. We were told later on that the damage was done by the Bihar earthquake of 1934.

❑

57

Changes in Survey Techniques

Geological Survey of India (GSI) was established at Calcutta (now Kolkata) in 1851 by the British East India Company with the soul aim of locating coal for the Indian Railway. Mapping of different rock types was a precursor to this activity. The Officers of GSI, mostly British, were moving by train to the nearest railway station to their field area. The onward journey to the area of investigation was performed on horseback, while the camp equipment travelled on bullock carts. In Himalayan areas, it used to be on head loads. The field traverses were taken on foot and the data were plotted on the topographical maps (in short, 'toposheets'), provided by the Survey of India, which was established nearly a century back in 1767 mainly to cater to defence requirements. The measurement of slope and direction was done by simple instruments like Clinometer and Brunton Compass. For detailed survey a Theodolite and Plain Table was used with chain and graduated staff for sightings. The calculations for latitude and longitude (graticule) of the surveyed points were done manually and plotted on the plain table sheet.

The survey methods and logistics remained more or less the same until the turn of the century, when imported automobiles started moving on the Indian roads. Gradually with some better road connectivity, the life of a field geologist improved marginally, although in the interior areas it remained the same. In the post independent era, Jeep[4] utility vehicles were procured by GSI in fifties and with that the mode of transportation to field areas changed considerably. The camp equipment could be taken in the trailer of the jeep directly to the camp site, if connected with a road or cart track, otherwise on head load in inaccessible areas. Camp equipment had mainly tents, folding cots, folding chair tables, kitchen box, grocery items and stationery box. The tents had different types viz. L-tent (large tent), having three compartment, O-tent (Officer's tent) having two compartments and S-tent (service tent, shouldary) having one compartment with single or double fly and N-tent (necessity tent). Single fly S-tent was used for kitchen and double fly S-tent for living purpose, while N-tents were used for bath and toilet separately. During the training period of officers, pitching of tents was also demonstrated so that he can supervise the tent pitching in the field.

4 Mahindra & Mahindra Company was established by two brothers in 1945 and they began assembly of Jeep utility vehicles, which could be run on rough roads.

More specialised Divisions were added to GSI from time to time. These included Geophysics, Chemical, Drilling, Ground Water[5] and Engineering Geology Divisions, besides the Petrological and Palaeontological laboratories. Airbourn Mineral Surveys and Exploration (AMSE) and Marine wings were added subsequently. Aerial photography was developed by the western countries and used in the World War-I for intelligence purpose. It found much application in geology and other natural resource evaluation in the post war period. During the World War-II the technique of photo-interpretation got established and books of Photogeology were available. However, it took some time for the technique to come to survey organisations of India. After independence of India, the first Prime Minister, Mr Nehru visited The Netherlands, and met his counterpart Prof. Schrmerhorn, who was previously the head of International Training Centre for Aerial Photography (ITC). He impressed upon Mr Nehru about the utility of aerial photographs for survey of natural resources for developing countries. Consequently, an Indian Photo-interpretation Institute (IPI) was established at Dehra Dun with Dutch collaboration in 1966 and officers of GSI were trained in the new technique. In those days use of aerial photographs vs conventional mapping technique in map making was hotly debated. As more and more officers were trained in the new technique, its utility became more apparent and GSI opened Photogeology Division at regional levels. The technique of photogeology helped in reducing rigorous field work.

5 Ground Water Division was separated from GSI in 1972 to form Central Ground Water Board (CGWB).

The space agency NASA of the United States launched the first Earth Resources Technology Satellite (ERTS, later named LADSAT) in 1972, introducing the new technique of Remote Sensing. There was again a debate on Aerial Photography vs Satellite imagery among the members of survey community. However, with better resolution and repetitive coverage, the technique of Remote Sensing got established and the name of Photogeology Division was changed to Photogeology and Remote Sensing (PGRS) Division. The name of IPI was also changed to Indian Institute of Remote Sensing (IIRS). The technique of Remote Sensing found much application in GSI, especially in fault, lineament, snow cover assessment and geomorphological studies. Indian Space Research Organisation (ISRO) launched its first Indian Remote Sensing Satellite (IRS-1) in 1988. GSI evaluated its data for geological purpose and soon a programme for mineral exploration was launched based on satellite data in early nineties.

In the meanwhile, US Department of Defence developed Global positioning system (GPS) which is a satellite based radio navigational system for providing positional accuracy in three dimension of any point. The technique was adopted by the Survey of India in 1990. The technique revolutionized the conventional survey by theodolite through GPS, Differential GPS and Total Station. The graticule of a point is measured and plotted on a computer based system to produce a map on desired scale. The technique of Geographical Information System (GIS) manages the spatial (graphic) data and its attributes through digital data base system. All this required digitisation of a large number of maps and reports lying in GSI repositories. Geodata Divisions were created in GSI for this purpose. GSI entered in collaboration with BRGM of France to attain the objective of preparing Bibliographic Database, Geoscientific Database, Mineral Exploration and Digital Cartography for map making. Now a good database is available in GSI and the metadata of the same is being shared on National Spatial Data Infrastructure (NSDI) portal.

With these advanced techniques, field work in GSI has reduced. The tents are no longer used, firstly due to non-availability of free open lands for pitching the tents and secondly the guest houses and resorts are available in many places now. Also the GSI compensates hotel rents to a large extent, while staying on tour. Now the tent life is confined only to remote and inaccessible areas. Present day geologists are heavily dependent on aerial or drone photography and satellite imagery interpretation with limited field checks. The rigours of field work are much reduced now, which attracted many lady officers to join GSI. There was perhaps one lady officer in Geophysics Division in early sixties of last century. Later on few more lady officers joined the geology stream but they mostly worked in the laboratories. The number is swelling now due to aforementioned computer based modern techniques. They are taking part in the field surveys, removing the gender bias in GSI.

❑